# KARMA

*In The Mist of It All*

# By

DAWNN POTTS-POOLE

## Author's Note:

This is a book of fiction any references to actual events, real people, living or dead, or to real locales are intended only to give the novel a sense of reality and authenticity. Names, characters, places and incidents are either the product of the author's imagination or are used fictitiously and their resemblance, if any, to real life counterparts are entirely coincidental.

Author's Rough Draft

*Subject to errors before the finished copy

**kar·ma**: *the force generated by a person's actions*

*Acknowledgements:*

Well family, this has been a very long tedious journey. Writing this book has truly been emotional to say this least. I've learned things about myself this time around that have been healing and inspirational, more than anything, I've learned how to enjoy myself more.

There are a few people that I must thank for all of their support, but before I do I must thank my Lord and Savior for blessing me and placing me just where I needed to be in my life. He is able and His Love is Devine, I am so blessed to know him.

To my boys, my young men, Christian and Quentin, I love you guys more than you could possibly know. Stay the path and God will carry you the rest of the way. To my cousin Gail, I love you cuz, and you know that. To Moses Jerome Poole, I WILL ALWAYS BE YOUR BIGGEST FAN!!!

And to whatever journeys the Lord has in store for me, Lord, order my steps.

"MURDER! Man get the fuck out of here, they got me fucked up. How the hell they gon' try and charge me with murder? Who'd the fuck I kill?" Patience cursed as he paced his cell, indictment papers in hand. "They got me fucked up," he snapped.

At that very moment, Dreamer and Knowledge were sitting at the courthouse where they had been since the early morning, waiting and wondering what was taking so long for them to bring him to court. Neither had the chance to speak with Patience lawyer, but both wanting to know what they could expect.

"Something's not right Knowledge," Dreamer said. "We've been here almost four hours and not one word has been said to us. Where the hell is Patience lawyer, he knows that we're here because he's passed us several times and hasn't said a word."

"I don't know what's up, I'm going back to the courtroom and just wait," Knowledge replied.

Patience lawyer entered the courtroom from the judges' chamber and ask Knowledge and Dreamer to step outside.

"Patience has another case and he should have the indictment papers as we speak. I can't give you any of the particulars, he'll have to fill you in, that's really all I can tell you," his lawyer said.

"What do you mean you can't tell us and what indictment? We've been here all morning and now he has an indictment! You need to tell us something," Dreamer snapped, getting hotter by the minute.

"You're his wife right, you'll have to ask him," Mr. Rodriguez replied.

"You're his lawyer right and you're here, I'm asking you," she snapped again.

"You'll have to talk to him, I can only tell you that this new case trumps the other three," he turned and walked away.

"What the hell!" Dreamer stood there in disbelief.

"Man," was all Knowledge could say. They left the courthouse in silence.

Dreamer returned home to chaos and disorder after burying Diamond, her death still fresh on her mind and now this. Patience was being indicted on another charge. What the hell else could go wrong and what could possibly "trump" the three cases that he was already facing? How had everything in their life gone so wrong? She mistakenly believed that if she gave him her all it would be enough, it wasn't enough, it would never be enough for him. He was never going to change and the sad thing was she didn't expect him to.

The last few weeks Dream's cell phone had been jumping and today was no different. You ever got the feeling when the phone rang, you knew who it was, but it hadn't ranged any different? Dreamer could tell in her soul it was Patience. She had been so perturbed about the whole thing that had went down at the courthouse that she wasn't sure if she wanted to talk to him or not, somewhere in all of this, she knew he still wasn't telling her the truth. She expected more from her husband, but now the rules in the game had changed, it was no longer jumping bail or selling drugs to a cop, he was being charged with something new and she deserved the truth.

"You have a collect phone call from..."yeah" the male voice on the other end said.

"Will you accept the call?" The recorded operator asked.

Dreamer thought about it for a moment.

"Are you still there?" The operator asked.

She pressed zero and accepted his call.

"Did you come down here?" he asked her.

"Try hello, and yeah, we were there," she replied dryly.

"Who the fuck is we?" Patience snapped.

"Excuse me, I'm not the one you need to be giving attitude," she replied.

"What? You feel like playing. Man what they say?" Patience asked.

"You tell me Patience. What did your lawyer say?" she asked.

"How the hell am I suppose to know, they didn't come and get me for court," he replied.

"No shit, I'm so tired of you. Why would I expect you to tell me anything different other than a lie? So you having another case does not surprise me Patience," Dreamer snapped.

"What other case?" Patience asked.

"You did receive your indictment papers today right? And you don't know what you're being charged with right? Why do I continue to go through this with you? Patience, I'm tired physically and mentally frustrated with all of your bull. This shit right here, I'm not up to doing this with you, so what's up? You want to tell me the truth or not? And by the way I think there's something I should tell you," Dreamer added.

"What's that," he listened.

"Doing you has been the cause of all of your problems including this mess you're in now," she said.

Patience wasn't going to fold. She was tired and he knew sooner than later, she would give up the fight, he just needed to hold out.

"Back to the indictment papers and for what?" Patience asked.

Lie to the end. This lying son-of-a-bitch still wasn't going to be honest. It took everything in Dreamer not to just hang up on him. Lie 'til the end, that was his motto and that could partially, no that was the reason his ass was caught up in all of this mess. He had to know that she knew about the indictment papers, maybe not what was in them, but she knew it had to be all bad. She didn't have all of the answers yet, but eventually she would find out the truth. She cracked half a smile and thought to herself, "Some things never change. It's fucked up, but if this is what he wants than who am I to argue with him, it's his life and he's been clear about that on more than one occasion." It was sad, but you always had to be on some shit when it came to Patience, she knew what it was, he had taught her well.

"Patience what are you being charged with now or are you interested in wasting more of my time lying to me and insulting my intelligence?" she asked.

"Man, get the fuck out of here! Since you seem to know so much, why don't you tell me what's going on?" he asked.

"Reverse the conversation I almost forgot how good you are at that. I don't know! But instead of being an ass, why don't you try telling me the truth for a change. Knowledge and I sat in that courthouse half the morning and part of the afternoon, but of course you already know that. Your lawyer, yeah he's an ass too, now I understand your problem with him, he mirrors you. He was in and out, here it was almost five hours later and he came to us and said that you had another case. I asked him what and he tells me I will have to ask you. So I'm asking you, why don't you tell me Patience, why don't you tell me what the hell is going on? I also figured out your lawyer's problem with answering questions from me, I wasn't the other fuckin' woman, but actually your wife, so he chose his words carefully, in order not to fuck up who he was giving your info to, such a fuckin' waste of my time, this whole thing with you. He seemed a little shocked and clueless that you were married, but I don't know why, by now he should know to expect the unexpected from you. So when he conveniently ignored my question about what was going on with you, he turned to your brother and told him, it was murder," Dreamer spit with disgust.

"Call him," Patience snapped.

"Oh, now you want to call him," Dreamer said.

"Call the lawyer..."

"I'd love to call the both of you something, but it still wouldn't change the outcome of what has already been said and done," Dreamer replied.

"Man, just call the fuckin' lawyer," Patience snapped.

"Hey, Mr. Rodriguez, this is Patience Jones. What's going on, I was supposed to be in court today, but no one came for me."

"Yeah, that's because at the end of the day, they brought me your file and told me that an indictment had been handed down adding to the other three cases and that you should have gotten your paperwork yesterday," he replied.

"Nall I ain't got nothin'," Patience said.

"I'll be to see you in a couple of days I still don't have all of the particulars on this new case yet myself. I'm going to try and see if I can combine the three cases, but right now, I don't have any answers for you on this new one, like I said, they dropped this on me at the end of the day, yesterday. I didn't know this was coming down," Mr. Rodriguz said.

"Yeah a'ight! Hang up man, they got me fucked up, I've been sitting in here all this time and now they want to come with this shit. Man get the fuck out of here," Patience snapped.

"Call my brother. Man, what the fuck happened today?" Patience asked Knowledge.

"Shit, I can't even tell you. Man that murder shit, they're charging you with it," he said.

"How the fuck they just gon' charge me with that bitches murder? Get the fuck out of here. What'd the lawyer tell you?" Patience asked.

"He had been asking for your file since he got there. We were sitting in the courtroom and he asked us to step out so he could talk to us. He wouldn't tell Dream shit so I start askin' him questions. He said he had just heard it from the judge they had some new charges and evidence against you and they would be indicting you on murder. That shit's crazy," Knowledge said.

"Man yall got to get me the fuck out of here. They ain't about to stick that shit on me, they got me fucked up. Yeah, a'ight I'll call you later," hang up, he told Dreamer. What's wrong with you?" he asked her.

Dream held the phone in silence and disbelief. So it was murder, but she still didn't know it was Diamond's he was being implicated with. The streets had been talking, but the things she had heard she didn't want to believe. She wanted to hear the story and the truth from Patience and by the look of things she wasn't going to get that either. When the lawyer wouldn't talk to her she had walked away, Knowledge had only told her half of the story. She held the phone and listened in silence as Knowledge finally dropped the name of the dead person…it was Diamond. Not knowing what to say, she felt as though a dagger had gone through her heart, her breathing got heavy and her chest filled with pain. She tried not to lose her composure, but she had to find out the truth, and it was too late to stop her rage of emotions, she lost it.

"You lying son-of-a-bitch, what did you do to my friend?" she yelled.

"How could your name be associated with something so ruthless? She was my friend Patience. What the hell is going on, I deserve some answers. Cut the games, real talk, what's up? What the hell were you into?" she was screaming at the top of her voice.

"Man you need to chill. I don't know what the fuck is going on. I haven't killed anyone and I can't believe you just tripped like that on me," Patience said.

Dreamer held the phone not knowing what to think or say, Patience had lied to her about so much that she didn't know what to believe, but what she did know was that the more she found out, the more it hurt and tore her down, destroying everything she thought she once knew about him. The Patience she knew was always unpredictable, but never anything like this.

If she could have jumped through the phone at that very moment it would've been on. "Was this what all of your lying and sneaking around was about? Is this what you do, who you are, is that the real reason you ran, you fuckin' took my gyrl's life?"

"Bitch, you lost your mind? That's what you think? You think I killed Diamond, that nothing ass bitch should be dead, but not by my hands. Get the fuck out of here, I'm getting charged with murder and could lose my freedom and all you're worried about is that nothing ass ho," Patience yelled at her.

CLICK! The line went dead. Patience had hung up.

Patience had spun so many lies that she didn't know if he was actually telling her the truth about his innocence or not. She was tired and confused about everything. Could he have done it and if so why? Was Patience that cold? They had been together forever and she thought she knew him best, but so much had been going on with him lately it was evident that he wasn't the same man. He had became distracted, edgy and secretive and Patience didn't keep secrets from her, or did he, would he, had he?

Her conversations with him were definitely strained and touch sensitive, especially after she heard whose murder he was being charged him with. The tears flowed even harder, every conversation from that point on only led to other altercations between the two. Patience believed his wife didn't and couldn't understand what he was going through and dealing with her lack of trust in him only frustrated him more.

They were beginning to say things that hurt and cut to the core. She accused him of being a liar and he accused her of not giving a fuck about what happened to him not to mention she was a liar and a cheater, he had nerves.

Three days had passed since their last conversation. They both needed time to cool off, especially after what was last said. Still Dreamer had nothing to say. What could she say? Murder and Diamond in the same sentence, none of this was making sense. What did Diamond's murder have to do with Patience and why was he being charged with it? Her thoughts were rushing a mile a minute and on the other end Patience's mind was doing the same.

His life had flashed before his eyes, where and when in the hell did it take on all of these awful events? Where in the hell did murder play a part? He couldn't admit to Dream that he understood why she felt the way she was feeling, he had lied to her about so many things, but she was supposed to be his biggest fan, no matter what and now something so tragic had made her doubt him and his word. A year ago, things had been totally different, but it wasn't enough for him. He was expecting his second child, a son, the one he had longed for and always wanted. He had came home trying to right some wrongs and he just couldn't get things together. The entire situation was complicated enough to say the least. He had gotten married and was trying to mend some fences with his now wife and be a father to the son he had wanted so badly. His intentions were good, but he hadn't thought it all through, he hadn't intended on hurting her, it wasn't part of the plan.

He had came home to a fresh batch of lies that he had created and was hoping to put a new spin on them before they had gotten out of control. Out on parole and he hadn't been into anything, things appeared to be working in his favor, but the moment he thought his paperwork had cleared him, the shit hit the fan. Now he had four cases pending against him and one carried the death penalty. What the fuck had happened?

He was kickin' himself as he re-evaluated the past year and what he hated to admit was what he saw when he replayed his life. If being honest was all that it took to set his life straight then he would have taken that choice over all that had gone down. He realized that he had treated Dreamer like shit over that past year. He had stopped coming home and was feeding her lies when he did. He knew his nights didn't end with hustling they ended with him in Shaunnie's bed most nights. He had disregarded and disrespected Dreamer's feelings for him and their marriage. The more she fought to stand by him and hold on to their marriage, the more he did everything possible to push her away. He loved her, but didn't know how to love her. Thinking back carefully now on all of the conversations they shared, he could see how it had lead to this fatal day. He had to admit that she was right about a few things, if not everything. She was definitely right about it being time for him to leave the streets behind, but it was a little to late for that now. That right there, he wished he would have listened too. Not only was his mind filled with all he should have done, it was filled with things he shouldn't have. He thought about how he had given Dream his ass to kiss, with his whole, "I don't give a fuck if you leave," attitude one too many times. He had flaunted Shaunnie in her face and used her to dig into Dream's hurt and pain.

"File for the divorce," he would say. "Why you staying, if it's too much for you, you know you can always go, I ain't gone stop you ma." His words were cruel and malicious, just as he had intended for them to be. He wanted her to hurt, but she still couldn't understand why.

Finally she had done what he had said for the longest time, she had filed for divorce. Fifteen years of loving him gone in the blink of an eye. It had killed a piece of her soul and he knew it, but he didn't care.

Not only was talking about a divorce painful and frustrating for him, with all that was going on, she had been the closest thing to him for years and she was the easiest to unleash his rage on. Now he refused her letters, took her off of his visiting list and wanted nothing more to do with her, she could never had been his biggest fan. If she wanted a divorce than that was what she would get and he would never talk to her again. It was easier for him to escape and hate her through the divorce, than to admit he still loved and wanted her to be by his side. Whether he wanted to admit it or not he was suffering from all the things that he had done, not only to her, but thru the choices and consequences he had made on the streets, they had now come to lie at his door.

Things had gone from bad to worse for him so it seemed, everything was a mess. He was scheduled to appear in court on three different charges and things were looking up at first, he wasn't facing that much time, but instead he was served indictment papers for murder. They say "when it rains, it pours," and "Karma is a mutha" those were understatements. If it was for no luck, Patience wouldn't have any luck at all. His tolerance for being back in jail only fueled his attitude still he had no one to blame but himself.

His marriage was pretty much over, the damage he had done he knew he could never repair. Dreamer had put on her game face and weathered the storm that had been dealt to her with a vengeance. Patience had put her through pure hell and had thrown her away, leaving her for dead.

His face had been plastered across the news and his name had been slandered in the hood. Local newspapers and petty gossip surrounded by lies were all that came when his name was mentioned. The streets, in certain circles had him portrayed as a murderer and a snitch. People passed judgment on him and they didn't know him and his so called friends and boys, they all road high on his downfall and she bore the weight of his pain because she knew him and this wasn't who he was.

Her friends and family felt for what she was going through and of course there were the bitches that were glad to see her down. "Be very careful bitches, the hole you dig for me is the one you'll dig for yourself. I'm a fighter and I know better than anyone, that when you're down there's only one way left to go and that's up, I'll see you hoes on my way back, believe that," she would respond.

Many people had a misconception about their relationship and what she could possibly had seen in him. Indeed, Patience was a bad boy for sure and Dream was very polished, what could they possibly have in common? Her years in the game, but there was a difference, she knew when to get out and she walked away without going to jail or losing her life to the treacherous game of street life.

When they were together Patience was a different man. They spent long nights talking and laughing with one another, enjoying each other's company and just the time they were spending together. The walks on the water, watching the sun set, holding hands and being in love, these were the things people didn't know about him.

He wasn't the monster they had made him out to be. He took care of her when she was sick, rubbed her back and feet after a long day at work and stayed home with her, just because. No, they didn't know him at all, they knew nothing about him.

Four cases pending and murder topped them all. Consciously knowing this Patience attitude only got worse, he blamed Dream for everything that had happened to him, it always came back to her cheating and not being honest about it. He failed to realize that he was responsible for his own actions.

"I'm going to ask you again, what's wrong with you," sarcasm in his voice.

"You're my problem. Have you looked at all of this? Are you seriously talking to me? You couldn't even be honest with me about your getting the indictment papers, why would I believe you would be honest with me about anything else, especially how Diamond ended up dead? I keep doing this thing with you, this whole, giving you the benefit of the doubt and all you do is continue to make an ass out of me for believing in you. Correction, I continue to make an ass of myself for allowing it to go on. Is it that hard for you to tell me the truth? Or is your life so fucked up that you don't know what the truth is anymore?" Dreamer asked.

"Man," Patience replied.

"When you came home and you kept your lie about Shaunnie a secret, why didn't you just push pass me? Why put me through all of this, when you knew you weren't going to be the man I needed? Why turn my life upside down with all of your drama? Why hurt me, lie to me and misuse me? And that lame shit that you're about to fix in your mouth, you know, I knew what type of man you were was when I met you, you can save that, it goes without saying. Don't be weak and hide behind that, stand for something or fall for it all. A person could never say that you're not consistent. Nothing has changed with you in fifteen years and that says a hell of a lot about the man you've become.

I, more than anyone wanted to believe that you had matured, I thought you knew what you wanted and I honestly believed it was us. I believed you wanted our marriage. You know what, I thought it was my fault that you weren't satisfied or happy, but I come to realize, that what's wrong is you on the inside. The outside paints this pretty picture of you having it all together, but you're totally fucked up, and what does that say about me, when I've stayed," Dreamer had begun to cry, he hated it when she cried.

"You done, get it all out so we won't have to go though this again. You done, are you sure you're done?" Patience asked.

"Yes Patience, I'm finally done," Dreamer spoke softly.

He heard her, but he wasn't listening. Something inside of her had snapped she had finally let go of him. She loved Patience, but loving him wasn't enough anymore and it wasn't going to fix their broken marriage, nor the trust that had been broken between them. With those words, Dream had made up her mind, she was leaving, there was nothing left to stay for, everything had been said and definitely done by the both of them.

"Look man, I can't handle you cryin', you know I've never been able to handle you and tears. I need you to hold things together, we both know this is some bullshit, right?" Patience asked.

Dreamer didn't respond. What could she say when her husband was being accused of murder? She didn't know what to say or what to believe. So much had gone on, he wasn't being accused of getting into a fight with someone, or hanging out somewhere when some drama went down, we were talking about murder and it being one of her best friends. If someone had told her he had gotten into a fight or someone had stepped to him on some crazy shit or ran up on him talkin' some b.s. and he put them on their ass, he had done that, but Patience was being accused of murder, there were no words for that.

Looking back on all of the lies that he had told, now running through her mind one by one, Dreamer needed and wanted to believe in him, like she always had, but this was different, there were too many lies and coincidences. She had always seen the good in him no matter what anyone else had to say, she never judged him. She wanted to believe that Patience was telling her the truth, but something was nagging at her gut in all of this craziness and it was hard to shake doubt when planted.

"I asked you a question," Patience broke her away from her thoughts.

"What was your question, you never answered mine?" she responded.

"So you weren't listening to me, fuck it, click over and call my Nanna."

"Who are you talking to like that?" she snapped.

"Man, can you just call my Nanna for me?" he asked.

Dream clicked over, dialed Nanna and sat the phone down. Patience as always had told her not too, but she needed to get her thoughts together and the more she heard his voice, versus the things that were going through her head, it only irritated her more. When she returned to the phone the line was dead.

**THE SETUP…**

Jeff, Patience, Bruce and Keyon were all boys, at one time. Jeff and Patience had been upstate together where they spent a year on separate charges. They hooked back up with one another once they hit the streets you know the saying, "birds of a feather." Patience had looked out for Jeff since he was released early, kept money on his books, took his phone calls so he could holla at his peeps, 'cause they didn't always have the cash for him to call home and there was nothing like being able to ring the house and hear a familiar voice on the other end while serving your time. When Jeff and Patience first started running together, Jeff fell back and peeped Patience's street game, he felt he was cool and he knew he could be trusted if anything ever went down. He also knew that Patience wasn't a snitch type of nigga and that's what's up, not to mention Patience treated Jeff like fam, shit was cool in the beginning.

Patience and Keyon kicked it around as well. If you saw one, the other wasn't far behind. Patience had been released on parole and one night while he and Keyon were hangin' out Patience got busted for selling dope to a cop. Keyon took off running and Patience went to jail, said he didn't run 'cause he hadn't done shit wrong, not the way the officer said it went down. He spent a week in jail and Jeff dropped some ends to help with his bail and Dream made other arrangements and a couple moves to come up with the rest. Patience seemed to have luck in his corner, again he was released, but the case he caught wasn't going to sit pretty with the judge appointed to hear it. Quiet as it was kept Patience should have stayed in jail, it would have kept him free him from the bullshit that was about to follow.

Jeff had Patience's back on everything, even lying to Dream a few times about his he whereabouts. Patience had been so pre-occupied with the drama he was getting from the wife and the baby mama's that his hustle had begun to suffer. Bruce and Jeff saw chance and opportunity when Patience started slipping and there was no time like the present to get even with him. Patience had done a lot of shit in the streets, giving him a long list of enemies seen and unseen, but none were brave enough to face him, they talked shit behind his back, but didn't have the balls to run up on him. It left him knowing that he couldn't trust anyone, everyone was suspect, but did that apply to Jeff, he was his boy, he had his back…right?

After bailing him out, Dream hoped that he would step back a minute, get his second wind and approach things with a fresh pair of eyes, no such luck. They say only fools rushed in and Patience seemed to take the lead, in the beginning he kept his court dates and parole visits, but it wasn't long before he got off track. He woke up one morning and decided he wasn't going back to court again. Bad choice, that's when the bottom fell completely out.

He caught a case in the Jects, thanks to Shaunnie, that scandalous bitch was on point when it came to getting him into shit, whether it was neighborhood shit or domestic. She was a combination of bad news and hoodrat wrapped into one. She was bad business from the moment they met; they were toxic like bleach and ammonia, the price he paid for thinking with his little head. Needless to say, everyone in his circle knew if some shit ever jumped off they could depend on him for backup. What Patience failed to see was that they all, including "the baby mamas" was just using him.

Shaunnie had started some bullshit, hit Patience on his cell and gave him the drama rundown, bitch started it she should have handled it. If he would have ignored her call, what followed could have been avoided. The bitch dipped, called him from her house, tried to persuade him not to go, she had covered her ass, but captain save a hoe was to the rescue.

When he made it to the Jects, tensions were already heated, some shots flew out and somebody got hit, he spent the next few days in jail behind that, him and one of his so called boys. Shit continued to follow him, going from bad to worse.

Allegedly one night he showed up at Chantell's house, the other baby mama and caused a disturbance. Not being able to stay away from her, she accused him of assaulting her, ripping her phone out of the wall and just going crazy, at least that was her story. Honestly, one never knew with them, their history was toxic and full of stories, you never knew who was telling the truth. Chantell had lied on him before, she had him charged with domestic violence, but later wrote a letter to the judge saying she had lied. She would have him thrown in jail just because she was having a bad day. Now with these latest charges, he would have to appear in front of a judge who had promised if he ever saw him again, he would make an example out of him. Not believing in karma, Patience found out that the judge he had just gone before would not only be hearing the drug case, but all four cases. He had found a way to be served indictment papers for a murder he allegedly committed, drugs he sold to a cop, domestic violence and parole violation, things weren't looking good for him.

Diamond's murder hadn't been something that was planned, it was an unexpected change of events that was triggered at the moment and Jeff hadn't anticipated on things going down the way they did. Keyon was a small technicality and the night Diamond was murdered he wasn't supposed to get caught up nor die, but Jeff couldn't take a chance, no loose ends. Diamond was something different, she had balls. She also had no idea that the four of them were boys and had been for years. For months Keyon had been fucking her over, in bed and out and she didn't have a clue, nor did she care, he was recreation and she was getting her money. Using was a two way street as far as she was concerned, fair exchange was no robbery. Truthfully the bitch thought she was fancy and to be honest, she was in every sense of the word, she had mad swag. She had stepped into the game and handled her business, but her cockiness and arrogance were another story. Not only had she gotten greedy, she had got in bed with the wrong brother. Her every step watched, her routine down, her money flow, calculated and killing her hadn't been an option in the beginning, just ruffed up a little and scared, enough to send a message to Patience, that his days on the streets and in the game were over.

Why Diamond? Patience and Diamond had decided to partner up and go in on product together, another something Patience wanted to keep from Dream. He always believed, what she didn't know wouldn't hurt her, he would soon find out how it would almost destroy her. Diamond balled with the big boys and she could hang as well as any nig on the street, she held her own, she talked mad shit and was able to back it up, she wasn't scary, none the least. You couldn't be scary when it came to this money. So when Patience decided to choose a partner, he chose Diamond. His boys knew why he had made the decision he had, Patience loved his wife and would lay his life down for her and in order for him to keep his street life from turning deadly and him having to eliminate one of his boys, Diamond would do.

She was getting her money and so was Patience, that's all that mattered. So when she dropped twenty-thousand cash and said she wanted in, hell he thought no more about it. They had established a mean understanding of one another, don't bring no shit to the table and there won't be none.

"Don't fuck over me and my money Patience, I would hate to fuck you up," Diamond had told him.

"Man listen, don't come at me on no bullshit, let this be your only warning and your last time talking to me like you crazy or you will have a problem," he snapped, gun in hand. His business with Diamond was exactly that and nothing more, but there was another problem brewing on the horizon, shit was definitely about to hit the fan.

The night Diamond and Keyon had their altercation it made for perfect timing. She didn't make it easy for them, the bitch just couldn't shut up, she was pissed and on a rampage because Keyon had supposedly been robbed of her money, making this just another problem for her to deal with and take back to Patience, this was the move that was finally going to let her walk away.

By the time Bruce, Jeff and a couple of their boys arrived on the set everything was up in arms, they sat back and watched as her gun was drawn and her anger was out of control. Diamond was heated, she wanted her money and if it meant putting a bullet in Keyon then that's how she would roll, but things weren't playing out that way. Diamond had a gut feeling from the start that there was some shit in the game and she knew that Keyon knew more than he was telling.

One bullet would cause just enough pain to let him know that she wasn't playing games with him, a flesh wound, two would let him know just how serious she was about her money and the third would finish him off if she needed to, as she saw it, it was all good.

When Bruce realized that Keyon didn't have the money, he knew he had to rush in because if he didn't, Diamond was going to kill him for sure and they would never find the cash.

Keyon held on to his lie about being robbed, a shot was fired and Diamond had hit him with a bullet from her pearl handled Desert Eagle.

"That's your only warning, a flesh wound let's hope the second one won't kill you. Where the hell is my money?" she yelled.

They watched as Keyon screamed in pain and tried to convenience Diamond he had been robbed, still she wasn't having it.

"It's niggas like you that piss me off. We had a good thing going but you had to try me. Keyon, don't make me kill you because sweetie I will, where's my fuckin' money?" Diamond asked.

Still holding his shoulder in pain and disbelief from the bullet that burned through his flesh, Keyon thought to himself, this bitch had gone crazy.

There was an odd calmness in her voice and as he laid there in pain he tried to re-examine the situation, hoping for a way out alive, but he came up empty knowing she wouldn't hesitate to kill him. She was getting more aggravated by the minute and wasn't feeling what he was trying to sale her and if he thought she had snapped with just one shot, he hadn't seen the worst of her yet. She held her semi-automatic pistol again on him, ready to unload, he could live or die, what the fuck, it didn't matter to her, she wanted what belonged to her and she would get it one way or the other.

"You must not have heard me, where's my fuckin' money Keyon?" Diamond asked.

Just as she aimed her gun to fire at him again, a Black Yukon rolled up with Bruce and Jeff and a couple other guys she didn't recognize.

Somebody jumped out and grabbed Diamond as she spun to aim her gun, firing off random shots. Before she knew it, Keyon brain's had exploded all over her. She screamed and scuffled with the person holding her, she heard Bruce's voice telling the guy to put her in the truck.

What the hell? Diamond was struggling to understand what had just gone down. Keyon had just beat her out of her money and now the muthafucka was dead, his blood was all over her and in an instance someone had grabbed her and she wasn't sure how long she had. Now how in the hell was she supposed to find her money?

Her mind was racing. "What the hell," she kept screaming. "Let go of me," she shouted. She knew she should have just kept it pushing and let Keyon's ass go, she had a stack of money and a ticket to Barbados in her purse, but she wanted what he had stolen from her, and now wasting time arguing with him was going to cost her, her life, she was sure of it.

**PICKING UP THE PIECES...**

Patience had almost destroyed Dreamer's life with his selfish decisions. He had cheated and fathered another child outside of their relationship, refused to leave the streets behind and now his actions had come to rest at their door. Still the thought of picking up the pieces and starting over for Dreamer seemed impossible, Patience had been her life. There was no denying he had put her thru pure hell and he didn't care, but whatever doubts she may have had, she needed to put them to rest in order to move forward.

She had survived the trials and tribulations of their relationship before, but now things were different. She had stayed committed to a failed marriage that was based on lies and deceit from the start, he had forced her into a position to make a decision, was their marriage worth it, more so, did she love him more than she loved herself?

Leaving was going to be one of the toughest things she ever had to do, it had always been her and Patience for the longest time, but with all that had gone down, she knew things would never change, same shit, different day, fifteen years later. He had chosen everything and everyone over her; there was no longer any room for her in his life. In all their years together, Patience hadn't learned that he didn't need to lie too her, that she would always be his biggest fan, but his lies had gotten out of control.

His life had been tossed and torn into nothing more than a trail of destruction. His habitual lying nature continued to follow him and Dream just couldn't deal with it any longer, it had become a way of life, a never ending pattern. She was strong enough to deal with anything, she had dealt with his cheating and on going infidelity and rolled with him, dealt with him spending time in jail and never judged him, but the real of it all, their marriage just couldn't survived another lie. There was no need for her to continue fooling herself, she knew better, she knew that as time went on there were going to be more stories, more lies, more pain and she would only end up hating and resenting him. Starting over would be hard, she was afraid and she would be alone, she had given her all to her husband but Dreamer knew she could never regain what he had stripped from her, something he had always given her, a sense of trust, his word and his loyalty.

It all seemed unbearable in the beginning, she wasn't sure if she was even ready, but the more she thought about it or looked into Drew's eyes, she knew that good things did happen to good people, as long as she believed in God and stayed prayerful, He would see her though. Initially she hadn't broken her vows, she was determined not to, and the wonderful thing about Drew was he respected her and he wouldn't allow her too. God always knows what you need and when you need it. He never let's you down. Drew's understanding nature reminded her of all of the things she loved about him, he understood and he didn't cross the boundaries, he didn't want to make things more complicated for her, he would wait, he felt she was worth it.

Drew had walked into Dreamer's life when everything was up in the air and a mess, where she couldn't see a clear path to anything ever getting any better. His being there gave her everything she wanted and needed, unconditionally. A total package when it came to being a pleasant distraction. He was a blessing and was everything she ever wanted and deserved. Drew kept her smiling long after he was gone, his presence lingered and just to hear his voice brought comfort to her day.

She knew how to survive and re-evaluating her situation was tedious to say the least. What she was willing to accept and not accept from Patience was at the top of her list, and some things had to change and come to an end. Had their friendship and marriage ran its course? She went over everything in her head, where they had been, where they had gone and where they wanted to be, at one time. She would have to continue the journey alone, without him. She found herself many days in a daze, alone with memories that could never be forgotten or erased, the good, the bad and the ugly. When he needed a place to lay his head, she was there, when he was running from the law, she was there, when he was beat down by the baby mamas and their drama, she was there. She was always there when life was taking on rough times, but now, who had her? He had jumped bail, went on the run and left her for dead and he didn't believe he was being selfish. He had always told her, he would always be just a phone call away if she ever needed him, it was something he promised. As she sat alone with her memories, it dawned on her why she always hated promises she felt they were always made to be broken.

Then there was Drew, who held her heart in his hands with such a gentleness, passion and love. He truly loved her, he always had. Drew was a dream that she thought could never exist. Not only was he handsome, smart, hard-working, full of ambition and drive, he knew how to treat her like a lady. He had spoiled her, they enjoyed being in the presence of one another and their chemistry was undeniable, one could tell that they were in love.

Yet the fact remained, Dreamer wasn't totally over Patience, nor was their marriage final. They shared a history, it wouldn't be easy getting over him, but it was something that had to be done, they had become toxic to one another.

They had lied and cheated, and Patience had begun to put his hands on her, something he had never done before. There was a incident one time where Patience was ready to kill a guy Dream had dated during their on again, off again stages, the guy had been abusing her and now he had done the same thing that he "promised" he would never do, not making him any better than that man.

They had been through a lot, she could remember Tori, her younger sister, once telling her "The heart can't feel, what the eyes can't see," but in Dream's case she had seen and felt far too much, for far too long, it was time to let go and let God fix all that had gone wrong.

She decided then, that she needed to grab a hold of her life, pick up the pieces and put them back together. Mercedes introduced her to a counselor and she was a little surprised, she had also given her the number of one of the top Black divorce attorney's, in the business, he was Fortune500's pick. Chance Winthrop, was partner in Winthrop, Weinberger and Goodwin and his track record preceded him. He was in top demand and now he was representing Dreamer Jones in her divorce. Her divorce, it all sound so surreal. Letting go and walking away would be bittersweet, but it was for the best. She could faintly hear Patience in the back of her mind, "If you love something set it free, if it returns it's yours." She had to let him go, in order for her to heal and move on with her life, divorcing him was the only way.

Dreamer had gone into their marriage with such happiness and high hopes. She never imagined that it would have caused her such heartache and pain. The counseling had been a tremendous help to her, and Stacy Norenberg deserved the credit. Stacy had not only become her therapist but also a good friend. Stacy, Mercedes and Dream had all became good friends over the process of her therapy. Mercedes had attended a couple of her sessions, lending her the support she knew her gyrl needed to get through this rough time.

As a therapist, Stacy tapped into Dreamer's world the way no one had ever done. She let her vent and helped her to see the light at the end of the tunnel and helped her to begin to understand why she had stayed with Patience for so long, she had became his enabler, always presenting the chance and opportunity for him to treat her the way that he did.

As a friend Stacy just fit in. Diamond was greatly missed by them all and her friendship was irreplaceable, but Stacy bought just her type of flavor to the table. They hadn't seen much of, nor talked to Shay since they returned from Barbados she had kept her distance after Mercedes had lost it on her when they were on the island.

One evening after a two hour session with Stacy, Dreamer picked up her purse and scheduled her next appointment. On her way out the door Stacy stopped her and asked what her plans were for the evening. Dream told her she was going to run by and drop Patience off some money, do some work and call it a night, the next day was a full one.

"So, he finally agreed to allow you to see him, that's good. Do tell, how did the visit go? And how was it seeing him after all this time," Stacy asked.

"No, I still haven't see him, but he said he was out of money and he need to get a few things, so I thought I would put some money on his books," Dreamer replied.

"When was his visiting day?" Stacy asked.

Dreamer stood there for a moment, wondering where she was going with this.

"Yesterday," she replied.

"Did he have any visitors?" Stacy asked.

"I'm sure Shaunnie and their son, were there," Dreamer answered.

"So why didn't she leave him any money?" Stacy asked.

"You know, I didn't even ask. Lately our conversations have been like walking on glass," Dreamer replied.

"As a friend…your conversations couldn't be that bad, he asked for money. As your therapist, Dream come, on Patience has been home for months, right, since they expedited him back and he has told you more than once that he doesn't want to see you, but its ok that you bring him money to the same place you are not able to visit him? Does that make sense to you?" Stacy asked.

"No, but just because he's an ass, doesn't mean I have to be one. I just want to be right, you know? I want the hurt to stop, I don't want to argue or fight, I just want the hurt to stop," Dream responded.

"My point exactly, be in control and stop the hurt and the catering to his every want and need. Try this for me, before you go in I want you to think about what we just talked about and after you go over it, if it doesn't make sense to you, than leave the money, but if it does, drive away and don't look back, cut your loses and that's not your therapist talking, that's your friend," Stacy said.

Dreamer stared at Stacy, "She couldn't be serious, could she?" But she was and Dream knew it. Stacy left Dreamer with her thoughts, but not before telling her she would see her at their next session and reminded her they were all hooking up at her house for dinner next weekend.

With Stacy words still lingering in her head, Dream drove towards the police station. Her cell phone indicated she had missed eight calls and had several voicemails. She knew they were either all from Patience or her office trying to get in contact with her. Stacy was right, Patience had been home for months and she hadn't seen him once. She had argued with him about visiting, but he had given her the same excuse every time, he wasn't ready to see her yet and when he was he would let her know. He was trying to grip his mind around all that was going on and trying to get a understanding of everything. He felt she couldn't understand how hard all of this was for him. The truth was he was afraid that she would run into Shaunnie or Chantell and there would be a problem between them or a problem for him. It was a definite that Shaunnie would continue to make his life a living hell because he had lied to her about being married. Dreamer was tired of the lies and Patience hadn't grown tired of telling them.

A half an hour later, she pulled up in front of the police station, sat in her car and gave Stacy's question serious and careful consideration. She loved Patience no one could ever doubt that, not even him, if he would have been honest. She would have never turned her back on him, she hadn't now, but she knew if she didn't stand for something, she would continue to fall for everything he continued to put out. She sat in her car a little longer, adjusted her rearview mirror and headed home.

**A STEP FORWARD...**

Having a better understanding of herself and her circumstance Dreamer had finally began to move on, but not before a final altercation with Patience. With all that had been said and done between them she felt they deserved a clean break and some healing between them. She was sure he would call. She hadn't left him any money and she knew when they did talk to one another, the conversation wouldn't be pretty.

A few days had gone by and no word from Patience, that was becoming a regular for him since Dream had practically accused him of murder; she had added insult to injury when she didn't leave any money on his books the other night. It only proved what he had been feeling for the longest, that she didn't give a damn about him. She had committed the ultimate betrayal of not holding her man down; it wasn't like she had done it before when he was sent away, but things were different this time, she was his wife and she was supposed to hold him down, right?

She had prepared herself for the worse, his attitude sucked lately and she was sure it was going to be even worse. This tension between them had been brewing for the longest, they needed to get things out in open so they both could close this chapter on their lives and move on.

Listening was something they hadn't honestly done in a while. When Patience finally called, he met her with the same pessimistic attitude he always did, but Dreamer wasn't up for it today.

"I'm glad your doin' the counseling thing and all, but I can't deal with this right now," Patience said.

"You can't deal with this, Patience how do you think I'm dealing with all of this? Van's been murdered, Diamond's dead and you're in jail and accused of it. I guess you think that I'm just living it up in luxury, right? Have you stopped just once to think about what I'm going through? In all your selfishness you haven't even ask me how I am doing, how I'm holding up? That's because you don't care. Our every conversation has been about you and what you want and what you need, what I'm not doing and should be doing for you. Damn, can I get just a little consideration, a little understanding? How about even a "Thank You," or "I'm Sorry" in the mist of everything you've put me through?"

"Man, here we go, don't start. You don't understand, I don't think you'll ever understand. You don't think that I'm dealing with this everyday? You think I want to be in here? I don't know who loves me anymore," Patience said.

"Why don't you help me understand? And damn, isn't that a slap in the face, you don't know who loves you? Is that what you really just said to me? Are you serious? Then tell me, what has my love for you been all of these years Patience, a waste of time? Damn. Let's just keep it real and call a spade a spade, it's not my love that you're questioning. If you have to question if other people love you, you need to drop that, I don't think it's working for you. I've never told you I didn't love you and you can't say that I haven't shown it, but I guess you just did. If it is my love that you're questioning, ask yourself this, how is it that you can't love a woman like me?" Dreamer replied.

"Did you bring me some money or what?" he asked.

"No, I want to come and visit you," she said.

"Nall," Patience snapped.

"Excuse you," Dreamer replied.

"I'm not ready to see you yet," Patience said.

"You're not ready to see me, but you expect me to continue dropping ends on your books and on the telephone so you can continue to call home? I want to see my husband! You're a piece of work, you know that? What kind of shit are you on? How long do you think I am supposed to play this game with you Patience?" Dreamer asked.

"Man, I'm not ready. How you gon' make me be ready for something that I'm not?" he replied.

"You know what, you're right. Take your time I'm done playing this game with you. You're afraid that I'll run into Shaunnie. She can come and visit, but I'm your wife and I'M not allowed to see you? You and that manipulating bitch are meant for one another, I've had it with yall. I got you, you don't ever have to worry about me asking to see you again, trust," Dream said calmly, she was done.

"She has my son," Patience replied.

"Don't. Don't be petty with me and most of all, stop insulting my intelligence. Don't use him as your excuse to hold on to her, she's gonna walk sooner or later and when she does, she's going to take him with her and what will your excuse be then? Like I said, I'm ok with this, trust. When you finally do ask me to come and see you, know for sure that it will be to late, because I meant what I said, I won't ever put asking to see you, out there again, I'm over it." Dreamer had said her peace, and she was done with it. Patience held the phone for a moment in silence, finally Dreamer spoke.

"So how does it feel?" she asked.

"How does what feel?" He replied.

"To be a ass?" Dream said.

"You talkin' a lot of shit right now, but if I was out there I would beat your ass," Patience told her.

"If I was you Patience, I would be careful about what I was saying," she said.

"I don't give a fuck!" he snapped.

"And that's exactly why things are like they are. I'm done," Dream said.

"So what are you saying that you're done. You want a divorce?" he asked.

Dream stared at the phone, she didn't respond there was nothing more to say, it was sealed and done. The initial sting of him not wanting to see her was gone and over with, it didn't mean anything to her anymore, she didn't love him anyway, right? She had already prepared herself, what Patience didn't know was the next time he talked to his wife, it would be through her attorney and she would be a brand new woman, one who would have gotten over him.

They were interrupted by the recording, letting them know that they only had a few more moments to talk, she hung up, there was nothing more to say, they had said it all.

Patience hung up knowing that what he was doing was hurting her, but it was for her own good.

## KARMA...

They say karma is a bitch and Patience was slowly finding that out. There had never been a time or situation that he couldn't get himself out of, until now. His thoughts, were overwhelmed the judge had just given him eighteen years on the four combined cases he had caught. His wife, who he had loved for years, was on some bullshit, or so he thought and Shaunnie had finally shown her ass to the fullest, being the bitch she truly was and could be, but he loved her and had sacrificed everything for her and their son.

What he had not anticipated was that he would have ended up back in jail and had his manhood challenged and belittled by Shaunnie whenever she felt the need. HE was in jail and it was his problem and she let that be known. Patience had taken his life and freedom for granted and now he had nothing but time to think about the choices he had so abruptly made. He thought about Shaunnie and what he wanted from her, he knew she was young and conniving, and could be lethal to him if he wasn't careful, but it remained, she was the mother of his child and he was willing to do whatever in order to keep him near. They had their moments and they shared some really good times together, for the most, she made him happy, but he knew she would never let him forget that he had lied to her.

Patience thought about Dreamer as well, more than he wanted to admit. He knew she was hurt by his betrayal and lies. He also knew she would have stayed if only he had asked, but his guilt wouldn't allow him to hold on to her and his pride wouldn't let him apologize and admit that he was wrong. By the time he realized that he wanted her back, it was too late.

Patience had fucked her and her feelings over so bad that the least he could do now was let her go. He didn't want to admit it, but Shaunnie was his reality, his choice. As they say, the grass isn't always greener on the other side, sometimes you had to water and nurture your own yard for it to grow.

He had put it out there to Dream that he wanted a life with Shaunnie and their son and it was where he wanted to be. Honestly for Dream, she knew it was the only way for him to be apart of his son's life. Shaunnie was a ruthless bitch and she used their son as nothing more than a pawn, she knew how much he loved him. "He's MY son nigga and whatever, it is what it is, you'll be ok," she would spit at him. She was nothing but a common neighborhood rat and Dream ways amazed at what her husband had chose to cheat with and destroy their marriage.

Funny, now that he had nothing but time on his hands, Patience was beginning to figure it all out. He was on his own as far as Dream was concerned, let it be his bitch's problem, he had left her for dead and went on the run, not considering the damage he had done to their lives.

Nothing had changed with Patience shit followed him to jail as well. One night he got into a fight on some old bogus shit. A couple guys caught him off guard and tried him, he got ruffed up pretty bad, but one of the other guys got a ass whippin' he wouldn't soon forget. The whole thing turned out to be a little message from Shaunnie to him with love. He eventually told Dream about what had gone on and wouldn't allow her to follow-up and press charges against the people who had done this to him. Somehow that night she knew he was in trouble and in pain, she could feel him. During the time of the fight, she was dealing with some bad stomach pains and didn't understand why, until Patience called her hours later explaining what had happened to him. He never came clean with her why the fight happened, but she already knew, she always knew.

Eighteen years, he had just freely handed the prison system eighteen years of his life, thrown to the wind, because he couldn't let go of the streets or a nothing ass woman. Now he was tied to her and the jail system. But it was all just beginning he had stood trial for murder, domestic violence and drug sales, what the hell else could possibly go wrong?

Before Patience and Dreamer had gotten married their relationship had had its share of on again, off again moments that either stemmed from him going to jail or them both being involved with someone else, only to end up back together. He had just came off of being locked down for two years and Dream hadn't held him down with lots of letters or keeping money on his books like so many other women had done and he hadn't expected her to like he didn't expect anyone else too. Patience could be stubborn when a person tried to be there for him or in his corner he didn't know how to accept help or constructive criticism because he was use to depending and providing for himself. Things between Dream and Patience were bad, they were in a place that they had never been before.

They always believed that their friendship could survive anything, now it had been tested. Patience thought about his wife more than he wanted to admit, but his pride would never let him admit that to her. The shit with Shaunnie had finally hit the fan, all he needed was for Dream to hold on to what they had and believe in him the way she always had, but it was to late, it had definitely destroyed his marriage and their friendship. He had gambled everything for Shaunnie. He had hurt Dream, and he couldn't deny the pain he had caused her. Patience expected things to remain the same between them, the way they always had, when he had done dirt and she was thee and would forgive him, but this time things were different. This time Dreamer had walked away the way Patience had asked her too. Patience could feel her sense of pain in his heart and he knew that she wasn't returning.

It had always been his pride getting the best of him and he would never let her know that he got played by the baby mamas. He had dogged and hurt Dream to the fullest, he lashed out at her, insulted her intelligence and hurt her feelings, tried to break her spirit. He wanted her to be at fault for his short comings and mistakes. Patience knew that Dreamer's love for him was true, he could never doubt it as much as he fault it, even now that they were apart. He acted an ass with her at times, but he knew he could count on her right or wrong, she never judged him. With everything they had gone through he wasn't sure if that was still the case, her believing him. He had put it out there too many times, that she didn't matter to him and how much he wanted her to file for the divorce, that their marriage was over, a lie from the start. It was true, he wanted to hold on to them all and in the mist of everything, he knew he would eventually lose someone. Dreamer was the best thing that ever happened to him, she completed him and now he knew it, but it was to late, the damage was done.

Dealing with her on an emotional level, now was something that was impossible. He thought about what she had once said to him, that he didn't know how to love a woman like her, maybe she was right, she was one of a kind that was for sure. She was classy with a touch of street, but only when necessary, intelligent, beautiful and had a swagger all of her own. She played by no ones rules and was always about her business, those were just some of the things he loved about her.

She had stayed with him longer than he believed and he knew for certain that once he was back in jail, she was out for sure, but to his surprise she remained true to their marriage, she would have rode this out with him, if only he had asked.

Before he went on the run, she had stood by him and once he was expedited back, she was their in the courtroom for all but two of his court dates, worried and concerned.

But now, the things that had been said between them had brought distance, hurt feelings and moments that couldn't be taken back. She had hooked up with some guy and really there was nothing he could do about it even if he wanted to. He had made it clear if she wanted to leave, go, no one was doing the time but him, he pushed her away. Patience had been locked down before and she had went on with her life, he caught up with her when he could, but now, she had pretty much kept her word, she was through.

Patience knew that things had been rocky for her he had put her through hell. He knew that she was hurting and he knew in his heart that she was taking this thing all in stride, but he couldn't get on that emotional roller coaster with her, no matter what, not when he needed to hold down the time he was doing and survive what he had been dealt. He had to detach himself emotionally from her in order to focus his every thought on saving his life.

Patience questioned her having his back, why would she? After everything he had done, his guilty conscience spoke volumes, he had done her wrong. Trying with everything in him to hold on to the outside world, he was slowly losing his grip and it frustrated him. Dream was getting a little more vocal and Patience hated it. Her mouth and words were lethal at times and could cut to the core of a brotha. She knew how to hurt him, with silence. She had away of saying nothing and it hurt.

Patience loved his wife…his wife, a word that he only used in private or when it was convenient for him, he never made her feel like she was. He knew she would be ok after all was said and done, but what he didn't know was that this whole thing had drained her. She was a strong woman and he knew she could hang with some of life's toughest moments and obstacles, he also knew he was her weakness and whatever affected him, affected her. Dreamer had begun to disconnect herself from him, her business was booming and things were looking up for her, she worked hard to have the things she wanted and it was about time that she enjoyed them. Though he would never admit it to her, secretly Patience wanted his wife back, but he knew eventually he would lose her, so it was better for him to shake her now. He knew that a woman like Dream couldn't be held down, not that he was trying to, but he didn't want to lose her. There was a lot that Patience refused to let go of and it had cost him not only his freedom, but his marriage, a love that he had had from his childhood. He continued to hold on to the baby mamas and in the process they both fucked him over. Chantell pressed charges on him for domestic violence and Shaunnie was just a bitch that gave him joy and grief all at the same time. But they were the least of his worries, his marriage was over, and he wondered if he had made the right choices. Dreamer had filed for divorce this time, distancing herself from him and the family that he, had never made feel like hers. He had made her feel like she was an outsider in his world and had sacrificed everything for his son's mother and it left no room for her.

Patience had a lot on his plate, dealing with the reality of spending a substantial amount of time in jail away from all that mattered to him. It had became a no win situation, knowing that neither one of the baby mamas would shed a tear for him, if he died tomorrow. Dream had cried for years for him, she hurt for him and he shitted on her in every way possible.

"I'm tired of being in here," he told Dreamer.

"Look, I know you are, but right now you're gonna have to chill. "This" all didn't happen overnight and it's not going to be resolved overnight. I don't know what you want me to do Patience, really I don't. You decided to let Shaunnie's handle things, let that be the reason I'm not doing anything else. And YOUR lawyer's incompetent ass, so really, tell me again, what it is that you want me to do? Let her handle your business, it's who you love and want, I think you should be giving her your orders and not me. So Patience, what role do I play in this drama called your life again, because it's far from being your wife. Shaunnie is the star, so what the fuck do you need me for, wardrobe? That will be a NO! Let that bitch comply with what you need," Dreamer snapped.

"Here we go again with your BS I can't wait to get home so I can beat your ass. She works and she has my son to take care of, she's not rolling in doe, she only makes $8 an hour, but that's no ones business," he snapped.

"Ok. So what is that suppose to mean to ME!? You were the fool to put your business in your hoes hands, let her handle you, 'cause trust, she's going to. I've tried to help you out of this situation, tried to get you to see the only way you are going to get out of it, but you don't listen. And with that mentality of putting your hands on me, you will continue to sit there. But anyway that wasn't the question, the question was…"

Dream began to say as Patience cut her off.

"Look, get me the fuck out of here," Patience yelled.

"Sure, when would you like me to pick you up?" she replied.

"You got fuckin' jokes?" he snapped.

"No, but it seems as though you do. I thought you would like that one. Have you seen your attorney?" Dreamer asked.

"Nall," he said.

"You haven't seen your attorney?" she asked again.

"I said nall," he snapped.

"I am so tired of his lying ass. Your brother told me that your attorney had seen you, spent two hours talking to you a couple of days ago. You still feel the need to lie to me. Knowledge filled me in on a lot of the attorney's conversation with you, but I figured you would stick to your motto, "lie 'til the end," no matter what. Part of the reason your ass is still in jail, because you continued lying, not only to your attorney, but to yourself and honestly Patience, that's the sad part, when you can't be honest with yourself. I knew that you've been lying to me for a while, I was just hoping that you would prove me wrong and come correct. Once again I believed in you and you proved me wrong and let me down," Dreamer said to him with discuss in her voice.

She thought about the day they got married, how happy she was, he almost passed out. She had once believed in their marriage and the vows they took. Patience hadn't changed; he was still a habitual liar selling false dreams to everyone. One never knew what to expect from Patience, his word use to be his bond, now it meant nothing when it came to telling the truth. He was subjected to lie at the drop of a dime and that's exactly what he did. She prayed that Patience would learn God's lesson, His life's lesson's before it was too late.

"You don't get it yet do you? You don't have to lie to me? Every time I begin to trust you I find out you've lied to me again. More than anyone, I want you to be cleared of this mess and come home, you're going through this for a reason, but I know there are still things you haven't told me, maybe not right now, for whatever your reason you don't want to, but one day, you'll tell me everything, and it will be to late for us. Things like why you really jumped bail and how you're being accused of Diamond's murder?" Dreamer said.

"How long we been on the phone?" Patience asked.

"Don't know," Dreamer said. Hell, he wasn't paying the bill and if he could lie why couldn't she?

Just then the operator interrupted their call, "You have sixty seconds remaining," Dream hung up without saying a word.

It was becoming more and more evident to her that Patience, though he was locked up and facing some serious time and charges, he wasn't going to change, and if looking at his current situation wasn't a wake up call for him, she didn't know what it was going to take. She thought it all was sad, how in just a little over a year his life had taken a drastic change and how he was back in a situation, he not so long ago protested he didn't want to repeat. The streets had pulled him back in and lived his life for him. She hated to see him throw his life away and relive this never ending nightmare. What she knew for sure, was that Patience wasn't half the man he used to be, because if he was, he wouldn't have been caught slippin' selling drugs to an undercover cop, doing eighteen years on a combination of charges and there would be no way in hell his name would ever by associated in a murder case, that just wasn't his m-o, or was it? Dreamer questioned everything now.

Still she found it hard to believe that Patience had been implicated in Diamond's death. She didn't know that this entire thing was supposedly planned before Patience went to jail, part of the reason he went on the run. No one had told her who, what, where and the when of it all. His family continued to lie and hide things from her, knowing eventually she would find out. She and Knowledge were meeting with Patience's attorney later in the week and she was hoping that he had taken a pill, pulled the stick out of his ass and answer some of the questions that undoubtedly needed to be explained.

Going back and forth to court was taking its toll on Dreamer. It was frustrating and she could only imagine what it was like for Patience. He had been given one of the worse judge's in the system to hear his case and it didn't help that he had a previous record to precede him.

Court dates were long, tedious and exhausting. Hours full of hearing other people cases before his and just sitting and waiting with no one to keep you abreast of anything. The judicial system cared nothing about you if you were a repeat offender or career criminal and Patience was both. There were days and hours Dream sat with Knowledge just waiting to get a glimpse of Patience, but there was no such luck. His court appointed attorney remained the same asshole from the start. The attorney that Dream had paid for and retained to handle Patience case had walked into the courtroom heard what the charges were and removed himself and taking her money with him.

She tried to hold things down and be supportive, but it was never enough for him. She kept money on the phone so he could call home at least giving him that sense of comfort, for what it was worth. She put money on his books, but it was never enough or fast enough for him and she was tired of him complaining. So it came as no surprise how he treated her when he was sentenced and she wasn't there.

Dream attended each of Patience court dates faithfully. The day before he was sentenced Dream, Knowledge and Patience grandmother had sat in court for nearly five hours when they decided not to bring him to court and postponed it for the next day. Unfortunately, she wasn't able to make his sentencing and when she received the phone call from him grandmother her heart seemed to stop. They had given him eighteen years and in just one phone call her entire world had come crashing down. The media, newspapers and gossip were the worse. The stories of what had happened and what surrounded the case hit the streets with a vengeance. Patience's so called friends turned their backs on him. The haters surfaced at full speed, Patience's life in the streets had hit home it was all bad.

Patience life had proved to be like an uncontrollable tornado, destroying everything in its path. He had screwed out in the streets and gotten a baby and a baby momma that was more trouble than she was worth having. He had destroyed his marriage and his friendship with his soon to be ex-wife and he was sitting in jail with four cases hanging over his head and murder had done him in.

Their world's stopped for a brief moment while they tired to figure out how to put their lives back together after such a tragic ending. It wasn't a death sentence, but it felt like it. Patience had never been sent away for this amount of time, his face and name had become notorious in the news and newspapers. One of Dreamer's conniving supervisor at the time who never had a good word for her or about her (always to her back and never to her face) had to audacity to ask if she was ok, it took everything in Dream not to curse her out, phony bitch. It was all she needed from her and her friends to sit around and take relish in her husband's misfortune. She wondered where those women were today, they no longer worked with her, be careful of the grave you dig for me, she thought to herself.

For months Dreamer cried herself to sleep. She pushed through her days like a champ but once she was alone with her thoughts her walls came down, not fully understanding where everything had gone from bad to worse.

## STARTING NEW...

Mercedes and Dreamer had been shopping the entire day. Dream had moved into her new home and she really didn't need to shop. Drew had provided everything she could have ever wanted. He had furnished the home in soft browns, gold, pearl and cream, her favorite colors and above her dining room table hung a beautiful Tiffany Crystal Chandelier that he had picked out for her while they were away on their trip, he had it shipped back before they returned as a surprise. Drew had spoiled Dream in ways that he had always wanted to, he knew this time he had to approach her in a different way, he had to take things slow. Drew knew that she was dealing with a lot of unfinished business with Patience and he didn't want to come across as pressuring her. At times, she would get a far away look in her eyes that she was thinking of, he couldn't expect her not too, they had a history together, not to mention she was still married to him, as much as she wanted everyone to believe she was over him, Drew knew that she wasn't. He was a part of her present, and soon Patience would be a part of her past. Drew knew she needed time to get over Patience and he was secure with that because eventually she would be his wife. The last few months had been hell on Dreamer. She had lost one of her best friends in a horrific murder and her soon to be ex-husband had been accused of it.

"Hey, what's up with you today, you've been quiet?" Mercedes asked.

"Just thinking, you know there's a lot going on, I'm meeting with Chance this week," Dreamer said.

"My gyrl, that's what's up, so you're going forward with the divorce? It's about time. I'm sure Drew is excited," Mercedes smiled.

"Drew is the least of my worries he's been great about everything. The man is unbelievable. He's making it hard, he's been a sweetheart through all of this. No pressure. I couldn't ask for a better man in my life. He has been asking a lot lately about the divorce, if everything with it was going okay," Dreamer said.

"Contrary to the way that I feel, I'll ask anyway, have you explained to him that you couldn't finalize the divorce until the trial was over?" Mercedes asked.

"I've mentioned it, but his response is always "In do time,". I've been vague with him about Patience lying to the police telling them he was with me, it would only infuriate him. We really haven't had the chance to sit and talk about things in great detail since we returned from Barbados. And honestly, I really don't want to, at least not right now. I don't want my life with Patience to become overbearing and overshadow what could be a future with Drew. And I'm just lovin' the attention he's givin' me. It seems like my divorce is going to take forever to be finalized and I have no idea when Patience trial is going to end, I'm sure their going to appeal the judges decision. I've shared as much with Drew as I can, which is little to nothing. Hell, I could be married to Patience for two or three more years," said Dream.

"OH HELL NO! If we have to go back to the Barbados, we're getting a divorce. No you're not going to give Patience another year of your life. We've been over this; this was his fault, his fuck up, not yours. Stop putting this off and put your needs first for once, what are you afraid of? Are you serious with this? Don't let this thing with Patience allow you to destroy what you could have with Drew. He cares a lot about you, and you deserve this, allow yourself to be loved.

Why do you put yourself through unnecessary hurt? Letting go of Patience will only liberate you and allow you to love a man who seems to have your best interest and feelings at heart," Mercedes said.

"Quit trippin', I knew that it was going to come to this sooner or later, it's just going to take a little longer than I anticipated. Damn chill, you act like you're divorcing him," Dreamer said.

"Hell, I might as well be. I've stayed up enough nights with your ass worrying and cryin' about him. I almost wrote him off on my taxes as a dependent, hell I need that. So what's the deal with Chance this week?" Mercedes asked.

"Timelines I guess. Get him the money and he gets me my divorce," Dream replied.

"So what's up with that? It's not like you don't have the money. What's up with you and Drew tonight?"

"Yeah, I have the money, Chance has been handling some other case and that's why we're hookin' up to get every thing squared away this week, in order to move forward. As for tonight, I'm not really sure he's being hush-hush about it. It's truly going to depend on my meeting with Chance. Plus, I'm still trying to settle into the house and unpacked I might be too tired for anything other than a hot bath and a movie. Speaking of Drew, I haven't spoken with him today he must have had a full day," Dream said.

"Concerned about your man, that's what's up. That's the Dream I know. You know, Drew was really concerned about you when he flew down for the whole thing with Diamond, I was impressed, not to mention a little shocked. You never really talked that much about him or how close the two of you really were, but I guess it had to be close enough for him to fly to Barbados to be by your side. I like that in him.

But I'm still confused. I just don't understand how you end up marrying Patience's sorry ass when Drew is a dream, no pun intended," Mercedes asked.

"None taken, I told you, Drew and I were a long time ago, we were at different points in our lives. I was letting the game go and he was enjoying the "hustle and flow," shit happens," Dreamer said.

"Seems like the two of you are at a crossroad again, and he appears to be hanging in here. So have you told Patience about you and Drew?" Mercedes smirked.

"Damn, you can kill a moment can't you? And to answer your question, yes I have. Lying has been the thing that's contributed to destroying our friendship and marriage, so I figured it wouldn't hurt to be honest, even though I don't know where this thing is going between us. At first, I didn't see a need to bring Patience into this, not that it really matters one way or the other, but if things between us, Drew and I are going to work, I have to be honest all around, you know? And I something really special comes out of this. It's not like it's going to matter to Patience anyway," Dream replied.

Dream fell silent for a moment again, alone with those thoughts. She thought about the time she and Drew were spending together and she liked it, hell she loved it. It had been years since she had felt this way towards anyone. It felt good not having to look over her shoulder or worry about what could be. In the last few months Drew had make sure that everything was taken care of, she didn't want or need for anything, not that she did, but he liked taking care of her. With every thought of him came a smile, she knew this was how she always wanted to feel.

Though she hadn't expressed it to him she was loving on him hard too. He made it known daily that he loved her and that she meant the world to him, and in many ways, it scared her. Dating had become something new to her. She had been out on a couple of dates with a guy she met when Patience was first transported back to their state, but it turned into nothing. She wasn't feeling the guy or so she told herself. She just didn't want to take the time to get to know someone new, so leaving before getting attached had became the solution. But there was something about Drew that made her feel secure, he always did. She loved how she felt in his arms, the way he took his time with her and allowed her to move at her own pace. The way he loved her and the way her feelings were important to him.

It was a wrap, in a few months her divorce would be final and as much as she wanted to believe Patience would be a part of her past, she knew in reality…he never quite would be. At least now she was in a place where she was open to the prospect of loving again. Drawing in from her trance, Dreamer said, "I still have to see this thing through with Patience. It's hard, you know I finally went to visit him," Dream said.

"Ok, now that you went, you've seen and you left, what? Don't trip and don't let Patience and his sob story draw you back in and you miss out on the best thing that has ever happened to you. The devil is a liar. DON'T START TRIPPIN', don't allow him to make you feel guilty either, Patience did all of this to himself, his ass wouldn't be in this situation if he would have listened from the start. What, now that Shaunnie has shown her true colors and treats a niggas ass some kind of way, not the way he thought she would, he wants to try and make his marriage work? HELL NO, that will be a NO Alex, cut the games. He had the chance and opportunity to make things right while he was on the streets, to show you how he felt and what was good between the two of you. So now that his bitch played him, dogged him and kicks him to the curb when she feels like it, he wants to come home? What price did you give him?"

"What? And who the hell is Alex?" Dreamer looked confused.

"Stay with me, don't stray and don't walk and chew gum. What's he willing to pay, let's see, Kobe gave up $4million, hell, Tiger just dropped more than that. DAMN, I forgot, HIS BROKE ASS CAN'T PAY FOR ANYTHING! He's broke Dream, just broke. You mean to tell me, a nigga had to be put on lockdown before he could respect home? Let it go, you did fifteen. I know you're not telling me you're going to wait for him?" Mercedes said.

"So much has happen, I don't know what to do, but waiting is not an option, so don't get yourself all worked up," Dreamer said.

"Loser! Lose the dead weight and the pounds he has you carrying," Mercedes laughed.

"You got jokes right," Dreamer laughed.

"**Real Talk**: Drop the dead weight, get on with your life, you only live once and if you allow nothing to waste your time, that's what you're gonna end up with, nothing. You're to beautiful of a person, inside and out to not enjoy life to its fullest. Let Patience have his bitch and kid. BUILD A BRIDGE AND GET OVER IT!! Mercedes said.

"I got you. Like I said, Drew has been a blessing in all of this madness he has been the only thing in my life thus far that has made sense, relationship wise. His confidence and strength have held me together many nights. And your right, fifteen years is a long time. I just want to make sure that moving forward with Drew is the right thing to do, I don't think I can take another rise and fall," said Dreamer.

"Damn gyrl, what happened to your confidence in yourself? Has that nothing ass husband of yours sucked you dry? This move isn't about Patience or Drew, Dream this is all about you, that's what's up. Trust, I'm not about to let you continue to down yourself, yeah, this shit has been real fucked up, but look at what's on the other side. Your business is doing great, you just moved into a beautiful home and you have a fine ass man that's willing to give you the best of everything, so can you come here with me, sign the damn papers and be done with it. You and Patience will always be friends, if that's what you want. Your marriage just couldn't work, didn't work, but it doesn't mean other relationships in your life won't, you just have to give them a chance.

Listen, I need you to be ready, I have to shoot to Miami for four days, so you know you're rollin' with your gyrl I'll text you all of the details. You know I love you ma, think about what I've said, holla at me later and we'll talk then. Peace Mami," Mercedes grabbed her keys and purse and was about to be out when she turned to Dream, "You mind if I take your car tonight, got a date and I'm not feeling the truck tonight," she said.

"You're rollin' that new Rover Onyx and you're not feelin' it? Oh hell yeah, I'll drive the truck, set the keys on the table and I'll see you in a couple of days," Dream said.

"Well it's a Benz night," Mercedes waved the keys in the air and dropped them on the table. She was out, leaving Dream alone with her thoughts.

Mercedes was her bestie, the closes thing she had to a sister. She and Tori hadn't been close in years and at the rate that things were going, they never would be.

Dream could always count on Mercedes and she knew she was right, she was always right it seemed. Mercedes had been better than her own sister. What was she afraid of? She knew she wanted to be with Drew and letting the past steal her present was out of the question. Whatever the case, she had to make a decision and there was no need to second guest her first mind, which was telling her to go see Chance, sign the divorce papers and get on with her life.

## WHAT GOES AROUND…

Patience had abandoned his wife for Shaunnie and in return, she had fucked him over royally. He spent more time arguing with her than he had with his wife, not to mention the love hate relationship they shared. She treated him like shit and he whenever she felt like it.

"Look Ma, I told you I needed to get my hand out of the lions' mouth, now that it's out, let's roll," Patience had told Dreamer.

"What? Just like that, forget everything that has happened and just like that we're suppose to roll? What the hell happen Patience? What did you find out? What did that dirty bitch do this time?" Dreamer asked.

"I told you, sooner or later if you give a person enough rope they'll hang themselves. I told you to trust me man, I knew what I was doing. All you had to do was trust me and let me drive. Eventually, sooner or later it was gonna be over with," he said.

"I want to know what happened and what changed your mind? I was right wasn't I? But it's never going to be over, no matter what you keep telling me," Dreamer replied.

There was silence on the line, Patience didn't reply. Telling her the truth still wasn't going to change anything between them, at least not in this case, so he did what came natural, he lied. He would never tell her she was right, never giving her that satisfaction. His motto was, admit to nothing, deny to the end. But this time, he had to admit it to himself, his wife was right, she had been right from the start, and though he was determined to keep the game going, he knew she knew the truth. But what he didn't know was that the more he lied to her, it built a wall that didn't trust him and she could never see them being together again.

"Look Ma, all I asked you to do was trust me. It's done it was going to end anyway sooner or later. Leave it alone," Patience said

"Why is it whenever you need to explain something to me, your best answer, your only answer is, leave it alone? Well I don't want to leave it alone, I want the truth Patience, for once can you just tell me the truth, or is it that you have lied so much that you really don't know what the truth is, or that you've lied so much that it's the only truth you know?" Dream asked.

"There's nothing to tell. It doesn't matter man, leave it alone," he said.

"This is what we're doing right? Expect me to respond to you like this in the near future and let it not be a problem with you accepting my answer," she said.

"You're petty," Patience said.

"And you're a liar," she snapped.

Their conversations had been bitter for a while, tonight they went there. Twenty minutes of going back and forth on nonsense. Dreamer believed Patience would pick an argument on purpose he needed that fight to help him through being locked up. This entire mess had been frustrating for the both of them. Neither knew how to channel their frustration and anger without hurting the others feelings, so they argued. Dream began to avoid his phone calls, as the divorce was going to be hard enough for her. She needed to detach herself from everything that reminded her of him. She threw herself into her work to keep her mind fully occupied. Since she would be taking a trip to Miami, she contacted a few of her clients and pushed a few meetings up, closing on a couple of ventures that were months down the road, putting her ahead

of the game. Miami was sounding better by the moment.

## WHERE DID HE COME FROM...

Drew was like a dream come true, Dreamer had always wanted a man like him in her life, and he was the total package and most of all, he wasn't Patience. He was charming and handsome, intelligent and well versed everything she remembered and loved about him still stood out and more. Don't get it wrong, Patience was fine, one the many things that attracted her to him, but Patience still had a lot of maturing to do. Drew woke her up to morning messages he would send, to late night conversations, he was slowly winning back her heart. He never shied away from telling her how much she meant to him and how much special she was to him. For him, her happiness was all that mattered.

The game had been good to him. He had his share of bumps and bruises, it came with the lifestyle and he had sacrificed a lot for the life that he was now living. It's was extremely comfortable and it allowed him to enjoy the finer things. He couldn't think of a lovelier and more deserving person than Dreamer, to share in his world.

Drew always knew that he had loved her from the moment they had met. There was something special about her and her laugh was infectious. Giving her the home of her dreams was just the beginning, he was going to share the rest of his life with her, no doubt about that.

"Hey, what's up?" Drew said.

"Hey yourself, how's your day going?" Dreamer asked.

"Busy, but I'm not complaining. Are you free for dinner tonight?" he asked.

"For you always, what's up?" she replied.

"Not much, just haven't seen that much of you or spent much quality time with you since we all came back from Barbados. I know you're tryin' to handle your business and I didn't want to crowd you, plus I have a surprise for you," he said.

"Oh no, no more surprises, I don't think I can handle another one. So why don't you spare me and tell me what it is," Dream asked.

"Its not tell you, its show you and you'll have to have dinner with me, agreed?" Drew asked.

"You're up to no good Mr. Davis, but I'll bite, I'll have dinner with you. But Drew, we need to talk," said Dreamer.

"I'll see you tonight beautiful, about seven," said Drew.

"Drew what's going on?" she asked.

"Too many questions, you trust me don't you?" he asked.

"You know I do, always have. I'll see you tonight," she replied.

There was that pause in the line, you know the one, right before you hang up and say those three words that always changes any relationship. Dreamer broke their silence.

"Was there something else...you wanted to say to me?" she asked.

He could tell that she had a smirk on her face and a smile on her lips. He had to approach this smoothly, he'd been wanting too tell her for months. But there had been so much going on and her divorce still wasn't final. He wanted to respect what she was going through and something's are better left unsaid for the moment.

"I'll see you tonight beautiful," Drew replied. He loved her, that went without saying and he never grew tired of feeling just that way, but if he stayed patient, she would be his wife and telling her he loved her would no longer be a secret.

## WHAT'S MY STORY...DREW DAVIS

"Yeah, I'm the brotha that made my living off the streets, the game treated me well and I'm thankful for it. It was a way of survival, not recreation, at least not for me. I say that without arrogance because I know how it can be interpreted. There's no cockiness about it, but it is what it is. To know where I'm going, you have to know where I've been, don't judge me. I've paid my dues for the choices I made.

I made my money and some smart investments that set me straight and that's what's up. This brings me to, how I met Dream back in the day when she was heavy in the game. She's always had swag about herself, still does and she wears it well. She's the type of dyme a man would have to be crazy as hell to fuck over, yet it makes me wonder what was up with that guy, you know her soon to be ex-husband, Patience. I have to thank him for dogging her, mistreating her and destroying her heart and the trust they once shared. It's given me a second chance at love with a beautiful person inside and out, allowing me to show her how a real man treats his lady. I love her, believe that and losing her, that's not even it, she's definitely wifey.

She's always been about her business and I love that in her. This thing between us has been pure chemistry from the start. Damn, she's sexy and smart, always has been, she works hard and her heart and spirit are good. Yeah, I love her can't say it enough, I guess I always have, those almond shaped eyes could mesmerize if only she allowed you to stare into them long enough, her sweet scent and the touch of her soft brown skin has me never wanting to let her go. Fellas, it's a beautiful thing when you can watch your lady sleep and know that she's resting peacefully without a care because you got her, I mean really got her.

Dreamer has always had my heart, we had a good thing back then, but I wasn't ready to let the streets go and she was ready to walk away, she always knew when enough was enough and leaving was our challenge. Now today, what's fucked up is that she's married to a lame who could never give her all of the things she wants and needs or deserves. The way she has stood by dude, many women would have been gone, but when she's down for you, she's down, so that's why there's no pressure from me, eventually, sooner or later, we'll be together, she's worth the wait.

Today she is still as headstrong as she was back in the day. I hate to see her hurting over this dude I want to give my baby the world or come damn close and it still wouldn't be enough for hall that she has gone through . Not many people can be dealt a hand like the one she's just held and continue to hold it together. That's what's up, she doesn't break under pressure.

I had been in the game for a few years when we met. I underestimated her ability to hold her on in this male dominated hustle, but she was about her money flow, and I liked that. What was even more attracted, she lived in the hood, but she wasn't hood, not by a long shot. Freakin' a mile or hangin' in bars wasn't her style. There was always something about her aura that spelled laid back and classy, and that she is. I noticed she spent a lot of time alone, it made me kind of skeptical about approaching her.

I decided to step to her one day and man, what I had once taken for arrogance, later I found was a confidence that made her even more attractive to me. The more time we spent together, I realized she completed me, after all this time she still does.

So tonight I'm taking her out to show her just how special she really is; she seems to carry the weight of the world on her shoulders. In a matter of months she's buried one of her closes friends, endured the loss of a murdered relative, stood by her soon to be ex-husband who has landed himself in jail and has filed for divorce all the while she's continuing to wear that beautiful smile. Her heart has been tested, her soul's foundation has been shaken, but damn this woman shows from every angle she is a survivor.

So yes, tonight is solely about letting her know that when she gets tired, I got her. She can depend on me and rest knowing that her wants and needs will be taken care of. I'll do whatever it takes to make sure she's happy because I refuse to lose her again.

Anybody in the game knows that the streets can make you or kill you, either way you make enemies along the road you've chosen. You never know who you can or can't trust you rely on your instinct and pray that it's right.

Dreamer and I were gamblers. We took chances and when things began to get to dangerous she road it out for awhile, she saw it through. But all of that changed the night I got robbed. $100,000 in a briefcase, I should have walked away like she asked me to. All I needed was three months and I was going to leave and take her with me. I went to meet my boys, shots ranged out, I was hit. She was devastated and the thought of her losing me that night consumed her, messed with her real bad, we were both glad things hadn't turned out worse. I tried to assure her that things were cool, but she wasn't hearing it. That night she asked me to leave the streets and the game, but I couldn't just walk away with unfinished business. She understood, but that night, she walked out my life, I hadn't seen or heard from her until I ran into her at the gas station. Its funny how life plays full circle, you know?

Dream not only left me and the game, she left the state. It had been years since we had any contact with one another so when I ran into her at the gas station that night, it was like being on familiar territory. She still looked as fine as she did when she walked away from me that night. I always knew she would be ok in whatever she would do. I just secretly wished we could have done it together. Now, since I've been given another opportunity, I gonna do it right. Second chances, you dig?

Getting her away for a while after Diamond's death was almost impossible. With very little leads it was making everything hard for her, there's been no closure and she needs that to heal. She doesn't talk about her, but I know she's on her mind, how couldn't she be, the four of them were like sisters, even though she's closer to Mercedes.

She began to wrap herself up in her work and wanted to take on the sole responsibility of what was going on with the house. I wanted and needed her to relax.

Tori and Mercedes were concerned about how much time she was spending alone after she would grind for hours at her office. I wanted her to have a place where when she felt overwhelmed and overloaded with life's issues she could unwind, so I purchased her a home in Miami on the water, it's her favorite place and like I've said, she deserves it. Thanks to Mercedes for getting her there this upcoming weekend, telling her she was going on business, I'll be meeting them there.

I figured I would take her to dinner tonight and surprise her with a few things, as much as I know how she hates surprises. I know material things can't replace or makeup for all the hurt and loss she's suffered, but I want her to know that this time around she's not alone. This time baby gyrl has a man that knows how to appreciate her. I won't rush her, just want to show her how she's suppose to be treated. I'm going to marry her; she's just that special to me."

There was something about the way Drew and Dream loved each other, it was unconditional. They could be in a room filled with people, but look at each other as though they were the only two in the room, a love for one another that had always been that way. Being able to accept each other for who they were flaws and all.

The open line of communication kept them strong, letting them agree to disagree while still respecting each others views. Though the years they spent apart didn't seem to have a lapse in it, their love for one another was refreshing and new. And now conversations ended with, "I miss you," or "I miss you more," both being just that short of saying "I love you".

"Who am I? I'm the man that gonna make all her dreams come true."

## WHERE DO I GO FROM HERE?...

Everyday was getting a little easier for Dream. She had begun to put her life back together and no was happier for her than Mercedes. It was good to see her gyrl genuinely smile again with a purpose. Dreamer had came a long way and having the courage to move on from a fifteen year marriage that had failed was a major accomplishment, when you had fault so hard to make things work. The reward in the end was some more gratifying, she had gained the love of a man that had her in every sense of the word. Moving on wasn't going to be so bad after all.

Drew was familiar and he had grown while they're lives had taken on separate missions. They both had a better understanding of life and its experiences. Everything they shared now was headed for longevity, there was not turning back.

"I filed for my divorce today. I sat down with Chance and went over my fifteen years of my marriage in an hour, can you believe that? A lifetime of memories gone in an hour, I had flashbacks of when Patience and I first met, the first time we made love, the baby we loss, our wedding day, our love for each other and then I had reservations about it all. This was my marriage and then it dawned on me, things had been bad between us for so long that I hadn't noticed when the "we" had became "me."

I closed my eyes and my heart still felt all the love and pain I had shared with Patience and it was a dark place, a place I know I needed to let go. But before I signed the papers, Chance must have read my face because he asked if I was sure and just for a moment I hesitated, but I couldn't forget the betrayal, the lies, the hurt and pain we had caused each another. I didn't trust Patience anymore and I knew it was something I could never get back, I'm sure of it.

"Van, I miss you so much. It's been two years today that you been gone. I want you to know, I still secretly laugh to myself about you telling me to throw toilet paper at her.

I have this hole in my heart that I'm not sure if I will ever be able to fill. Drew is trying really hard, he's loving and patient with me and I want to love him back because I do love him," Dreamer said.

"Patience has always been your weakness Princess. Drew seems to be a dream gyrl and you would be crazy to let him go, live a little pumpkin head, you only live once and gyrlll when your dead, you're dead, believe me, I know.

You know Mercedes is right. Allow someone to take care of you, and if Drew isn't your flavor, hell hook up with that attorney of yours, he's fine as hell, is he single?

Listen MaryKay, throw yourself a party, be happy that you've let go of what has been no good for you. Let Drew take you away for a few days, hell a week if you need the time and enjoy the moment. Throw yourself a Divorce Party and ba-by live.

The hardest part for you is over, walking away and not looking back is going to get easier, day by day.

Princess you know I love you, but you are making this thing harder by not just letting go. You can't keep what doesn't want to be kept and Patience has never been the kept type. You knew what you were getting when you married him. You loved him, now let him go, because if you're honest with yourself, he let go a long time ago.

You know I believe in living life to the fullest and I did right up to the end. Don't let a broken dream or a mission not complete detour you, start a new one," Van told her. He loved Dream and her happiness had always meant the world to him.

"I miss you more than you could ever know. Your being gone hasn't been easy on any of us, but I think it's been the hardest on me. I get lonely and I wish you were here to talk too, that shoulder I could cry on. I love you Van," she whispered.

She had those moments, when things got stressful or to much for her to handle she talked to him and for her it was like him being there. He still, always answered. He had become her comfort zone in the mist of life's overwhelming and crazy moments.

Drew was picking her up at seven and she hadn't begun to pack for her trip to Miami with Mercedes, but that was going to have to wait she needed to get a move on it, she knew he was prompt and she also knew how he hated to wait. He wasn't to specific about what they were doing tonight, other than dinner, but knowing Drew he had something up his sleeve that was bound to be extravagant, so she decided to pack her LV overnight bag just in case. He did mention they would check out the Chicago Ballroom dancing scene tonight since he knew she wanted to learn.

Dreamer pulled out a red halter dress, with a silver hoop at the bust line giving a little cleavage and her silver Rise Bread heels from Kenneth Cole. She pinned her hair up and jumped in the shower.

Forty-five minutes later she stood in her bathroom staring in the mirror. Who was she now? She looked the same, but who was she? She had been Dreamer Jones, wife of Patience Jones for fifteen years. She was intelligent, smart, well versed, ambitious, full of life and drive and she was starting again.

She hadn't heard from Patience since he was sentenced and sent away. The last time she had spoken to him was in the form of a letter saying she had left him for dead and hadn't stood by him. That she didn't mean shit to him and please file for the divorce, she was holding up his life. What the hell? She was hurt by what he had said, but she knew she was definitely done. Mercedes had wild out when she read the letter. Patience had expected her to jump ship from the start, but was surprised that she had stayed and was supportive as long as she had been.

"How in the hell did that nothing ass, soon to be ex-husband of yours really have the balls to say this bullshit? I'm surprised he was able to write it on paper since bullshit always came out of his mouth, he took a moment from jacking off, the muthafucka. Are you serious? Who the hell was keeping money on his books so that he could call home and not only talk to you but half of his family and should we not mention that dusty hoe Shaunnie that he wanted everybody to like and accept. Give a bitch a baby and I guess she's suppose to be in, dumb ass. I guess eventually she will wear on them. What was it, a bill every week if not more? What about the fucked up lawyer he insisted on having and you paid the retainer for and when he went to court he dropped the case as soon as he found out what type of fucked up situation he had gotten himself into this time, but of course he kept the damn money, that was honorable as fuck.

Shall I continue? What about all the times you showed up for court and they didn't bring him and you spent the day sitting that was a waste. You could have been handling your business, but you were there for him, showing support for his bitch ass. And don't get me started on all of the collect phone calls you accepted and put on your credit card so he could call home, but you left him for dead? FUCK HIM! You should have left. You weren't there for him? You shouldn't have been.

Patience wasn't use to shit when you first started fuckin' with him and when you hooked up, his sorry ass still didn't know what to do with you. I told you, he wasn't shit but a loser. After all that he's been through, his nothing ass couldn't write you a letter to say "Thank You" for being there for me and putting up with ALL my bullshit, no that was to much like right.

So he sends a letter filled with venom to hurt you even more? Who does that? I'm glad he's gone somewhere, anywhere other than here with you, now you can get on with your life. Damn if this doesn't get Drew a chance with you, I don't know what it's going to take," Mercedes said.

She was heated, no one better than her knew what Dream had been through with Patience. So when she stopped by earlier to pick up some papers, she keyed in and found Dream sitting at the island in the kitchen nursing Petron in the middle of the day, she knew something was wrong. The bottle was near empty and she had that, damn you Patience look on her face.

She confirmed her suspicions when she walked over to the glass table and dropped her keys and saw the letter from him lying there. Dream didn't move, she continued holding her glass and staring out the sliding glass doors to her patio, focusing on nothing in particular.

"Hey ma, you ok," Mercedes asked.

"Was I a bad wife or did I love him to much to not see this coming? Or was it that I saw it and I didn't want too?" Dream asked somewhat in a daze.

"Gyrl listen, Patience has nothing but time on his hands to fuck with you, he ain't going no where no time soon and if he thinks he can make you feel guilty, he's going to run with it. He has always been about self no matter how much he gave you, he took more back in return, which by looking at things in their current state, let's me know he could have kept it because it wasn't worth the headache.

He never knew how to love you even from the moment you guys met he wasn't use to a woman. You can't blame yourself for his shortcomings, but blame yourself for your choice in men. He looked good in clothes, but once you undressed him, he was a package of bullshit. Let him go and it's ok to do so, you feel me? The two of you may have come from the same hood, but you have always been from two different worlds and as much as I know you don't want to hear this, you're my gyrl and we keep it one hundred. He's street, always has been and that's the only type of woman he can be comfortable with. Yeah, you're a little hood, but you're not hood enough boo.

Your beaugie ass can and should only fuck with a thug for recreation and not relationship, if that's what you choose, a real thug, not a wannabe.

Drew is an exception to the rules. He's intelligent, well rounded and well versed. Papi's versatile and that's the type of brotha you need in your corner. Not the one in the corner wanting to get out and don't have a clue how to.

Mamie, the best thing you can do is let Chance rush this divorce and enjoy the ride to come. Since Patience balls and pride stopped him from saying thank you, bow out gracefully, real talk," Mercedes said.

"That's why you're my bestie. I can always count on you to kick me when I'm down, damn," Dreamer laughed.

"Seriously, I was surprised to see that he felt that way," Dream said.

"Why? He's been pulling shit like this for years. You say you know him best then nothing he does should surprise you. Look, I didn't stop by here for a drama session I needed to pickup some papers I left. Got em, try and have a nice time with Drew tonight and don't bring down the mood thinking about Patience, trust, he's not thinking about you, later ma," Mercedes said walking out the door.

Dream had been in the bathroom so long that she had taken a seat alone with her thoughts. A small smile rose from her lips as she thought about Drew. Good men do exists and she had one in Drew. Kem's "Share My Life," was blasting through the Bose surround sound system and she felt good for the first time in a longtime. She looked at the dress lying on her bed, then walked over to her closet and stood looking at the beautiful work Drew had done with his own hands. So much love had been put into her new home and she had him to thank. He had given her everything she had asked for and everything she hadn't. When she looked around her home she saw the both of them and it was comfortable, not strained or stressed. It was a small piece of heaven and she was enjoying it.

Dream looked at the time she had a half hour to get ready and she needed to be on time, tonight she didn't want Drew to have to wait for her, but she took in ten minutes more of what home really felt like when it was filled with love.

Dream has just finished the final touches to her dress and makeup, which she didn't wear, when she heard the alarm on the house disarm, Drew had let himself in.

"Hey love, wow you look nice. What's the occasion? That's right you have a date tonight with a very handsome man. I also heard that he's crazy about you," Drew winked.

"Than you better get out of here, because I don't want to mess this up," she said with a smile.

"Yeah, baby there has kind of been a change in our plans for tonight. I know I promised I would take you dancing, but I have to leave town in the morning, early. So dinner is all that we will be able to do tonight if that's ok with you," Drew said.

"Drew come on, you promised and you had me all excited for a night of surprises, I was looking forward to it," she said.

"I thought you didn't like surprises," he smiled. "Something unexpected came up and I have to fly out in the morning, I'll be gone a couple of days, but I promise when I get back you'll have that surprise and that special moment, promise. Have I ever broken a promise to you?" he asked.

"Yes, you just did. I want to be upset with you but I can't. I know spare of the moment leaving comes with the job, but you had me all excited about tonight. You know what, don't worry about it. Mercedes and I are going to Miami for a few days and I have business there that I've pushed dates up so it's ok. I'm not upset and it won't be that bad, plus I need to make this an early night because I still haven't packed," Dream said a little disappointed.

Drew dropped Dream off around one and she had a 6 a.m. flight and Mercedes was on her way. She didn't get to bed until 4a.m. so sleeping on the flight was definitely a yes. She had asked Mercedes to stop by McDonalds and pick up a large Carmel Latte she was going to need it.

Mercedes looked flawless. D & G was the flavor of the day and she had on a pair of shoes she had bought on their last trip to Miami from DASH.

"Ok, who is he?" Dream teased.

"A client who pays well for me to investigate his lying wife who he thinks is only out for his money. But so far his problem isn't her taking his money, but her cheating with a woman," Mercedes hollered.

"Gyrl shut the front door. What the....I guess that's going to be a kicker for him," Dream said.

"No the kicker is when the wife finds out he's leaving her for his man," Mercedes was in tears.

"I don't want to know any more, I don't think my heart can stand it," they both couldn't stop laughing.

"So how was the date last night with Drew?" Mercedes asked.

"Cut short," she replied.

"What did you do?"

"Why did it have to be me?"

"Because when I left here yesterday, you were feeling some sort of way about the letter you had got from you know who."

"Well that wasn't an issue. Drew had to leave on business this morning, something came up. So we went to dinner and what was supposed to be an early night for me turned into 1 a.m. And of course you know I had to pack," Dream said.

"So where's Mr. Wonderful off to now?" Mercedes asked.

"You know, I don't know. When he told me he was leaving, I didn't even ask. Well wherever it is, he'll be gone for a couple of days," said Dreamer.

"Someone sounds like they're going to miss him," Mercedes smiled.

"He's growing on me," Dream replied.

"Puppies grow on you. You're starting to feel him a little more, I can see it in your eyes," Mercedes smirked.

"That's the glare from my contacts you see," Dreamer laughed.

"Oh you got jokes, now I know my eyes don't deceive me. Hey we better get out of here. I called a car to pick us up. I'm not giving the airport another damn dime to baby sit my vehicle for four or five days," Mercedes chimed pulling her bags from the trunk of the truck.

Traffic was crazy getting to the airport and once they arrived they waited another hour in line to check in. Ever since 911 traveling by air had been pure hell, but you wanted to be safe.

Once they had boarded and settled in Dream fell straight off to sleep. The last time she had boarded a plane and touch down in Miami was when they connected a flight from there to Barbados to identify Diamonds body. She tossed and turned for a moment, it was the last time she had seen her friend and it wasn't the way she wanted to remember her.

Their flight was a comfortable one, it was a beautiful 89 degrees and the air was thick. They both couldn't wait to get to their hotel to shower and unwind before grabbing a bit to eat and doing a little shopping. You don't come to Miami and don't club or shop, it's against all the rules.

## THE START OF SOMETHING BEAUTIFUL...

"Listen Mami, I have a few errands to run, but let's hook up for lunch. Ah say about 1o'clock at Perricone's Marketplace, you know the spot right," Mercedes ask Dream as she dropped her bags and headed for the shower.

"Sure, but where are you off to in such a rush?" Dream asked.

"I'm meeting the guy I told you about, the one with the wife issue. Well he moved the time up because he has plans for tonight and he wants what I have so far, so I'm meeting him at his condo," Mercedes said.

"Ok, so 1o'clock it is. I'm going to check in with my clients to make sure we're still on schedule for our appointments today, and I'll get with you later," Dreamer said.

Dream checked her messages and returned some phone calls. She tried to get in a little work but was having a hard time. She hadn't heard from Drew yet and she wasn't sure if he had made it safely to wherever it was he was going.

She tried his cell, but it went straight to voicemail, which was a little unusual for him. She left a message before she showered and got dressed to meet Mercedes. Perricone's was absolutely beautiful, inside and out. She was escorted to her sit and told the waitress that she was expecting another person. She took in the scenery as she sipped on a glass of wine.

Her cell phone rang, it was Mercedes.

"Hey gyrl where are you? The old guy didn't try and make the moves on you did he?" Dreamer laughed.

"He or his boyfriend wouldn't know what to do with me, cause ba-by when I finished with them they would have stories to tell that no one would ever believe," Mercedes giggled.

"So what's up? How long before you get here?" Dream asked.

"That's why I'm calling. I'm not going to make it, I'm sorry ma, this is taking a little longer than I anticipated, but I'll catch you up on things back at the hotel," she said.

"Now what am I suppose to do? I'm in this beautiful restaurant and I have nothing to do. I was hoping you were gonna show so we could kick it for a little while," Dreamer said.

"I know, I'm sorry, but I promise we'll go out tonight. I don't have to meet him again until tomorrow afternoon and a gyrl can get in a couple of drinks and not worry about getting up bright and early. Since you're there stay and have lunch, enjoy the scenery and relax a little," Mercedes said.

"I hear ya, handle you business. I can stand some lunch and a little sight seeing and light shopping won't hurt. Catch up with you later," Dream hung up.

She sat for a moment looking at the menu when her hostess came over with another glass of wine. She looked a little confused. "I didn't order a second glass of wine," she said.

The waitress replied, "There's a gentleman sitting at the bar on the opposite end and he asked that I bring you another glass of what you were drinking, he's sitting right…that's funny, he's gone. Would you like me to take it back?"

"Yes, please," Dream replied.

As her waitress walked away, the gentleman who ordered the drink reappeared and asked why she was returning the drink. She told him that the lady refused to accept it. He took the glass from her and walked in Dream's direction, her back was faced to him. "Excuse me beautiful, but I'm a little offended that you wouldn't accept my drink, so I decided to bring it over myself and be rejected face to face," the male voice said.

For a moment Dreamer thought she was hearing things, couldn't be. As she slowly turned towards the voice, she couldn't believe her eyes, there stood Drew looking finer than ever and not only holding her glass of wine but a dozen of the most beautiful black roses she had ever seen. Black roses were Dreamer's favorite.

"Drew, what are you doing here?" Surprise in her voice and in her eyes.

He placed the glass and roses on the table, pulled her to her feet and kissed her like they had never kissed before. She was breathless when they finally broke away. Drew pulled her chair out as Dreamer sat back down. Still in shock and trying to catch her breath, she finally got it out, "What are you doing here, I thought you were away on a business trip?"

"My business was here in Miami, I wrapped it up this morning. Why, you're not happy to see me?" Drew joked.

"Of course I am, but why didn't you tell me? Wait a minute, how did you know where to find me?" Dreamer asked.

"I called Mercedes because you weren't answering your phone," he said.

"I tried calling you earlier, but it went straight to voicemail," she replied.

"That may be so I was in the middle of my meeting so my phone was shut off. I have something for you, we'll call it surprise number one," Drew said.

"Surprise number one," she looked confused.

"I made the reservations for lunch here two months ago, getting a table was a little difficult but you know how I am when I want something." he said with a seriousness in his tone.

Perricone's was your classic Italian Restaurant in downtown Miami. The café sat in a park on Brisckell Avenue. Inside they were surrounded by a beautiful landscape of trees where it was like walking through an erotic rainforest. The scenery on the outside was breathtaking, but once inside you're captivated in beauty.

"When did you have time? Drew this place is beautiful, I was just telling Mercedes that when she called and said she couldn't meet me here because her meeting was running over," Dreamer paused.

Mercedes…she shook her head and smiled. Her gyrl had set her up, in a good way. She knew all this time and I bet there's no old guy, Dreamer thought. Drew interrupted where she had gone in silence.

"I still know some people, who know some people. I figured you would enjoy this and we had been everywhere else, plus tonight is special," Drew said.

Dream looked at him and could see a sparkle in his eyes. "What's so special about tonight?" she asked.

"I made an investment today, but we can talk about that later, first let's get to our table. You see anything on the menu that catches your eyes? He asked.

"Are you kidding? Where do you want me to start?" She laughed.

The waitress approached their table and introduced herself again, "Good afternoon my name is Karmen and I will be your waitress. Can I freshen up your drink, and get you something sir?"

As their waitress took their drink order, Dreamer couldn't help staring at Drew, he was fine and amazing.

"Penny for your thoughts," he smiled.

He had the sexiest dimples and a killer smile. "You're unbelievable, thank you," she said.

"For what?" Drew asked.

"For being here and loving me, the way that you do," Dreamer said.

"You deserve these things and if I can continue to give them to you, I will," he said.

Before Dream could reply their waitress had returned with their drinks and was ready to take their orders. They ordered the Seafood Linguine w/sautéed Gulf shrimp, ocean scallops, mussels and calamari in fresh Scampi sauce for an appetizer.

Drew had Perricone's Classic Coppino – Shrimp, mussels, scallops, fresh Ahi Tuna and Salmon medallions over a bed of linguine with a seafood broth.

Dreamer ordered – Perricone's Portobello Mushroom Torta – Grilled Portobello mushroom, Prosciutto di Parma, grilled eggplant, vine ripened tomato, melted Fontina cheese, and drizzled with an aged balsamic vinegar and extra virgin olive oil, finished with their Signature Pomodoro sauce.

And for desert they shared a slice of Perricone's Chocolate House Cake – Chocolate cake drizzled with white chocolate, hazelnut crunch, rich bittersweet chocolate mousse with chocolate ganache frosting.

She would definitely have to hit the gym for sure after this. As they waited for their entrees Drew shared his day with her and she talked about the upcoming trip to Barbados and having to relive Diamond's last days leading up to her death.

Drew wanted to take her mind off of it, but knew it was no use. Shay hadn't been around much lately and she and Mercedes were still on bad terms and Dream wasn't a big fan of hers right now either.

"That scandalous bitch knew Diamond was in trouble and didn't say a word. Any other time, the trick couldn't hold water, but how do you let your gyrl end up fuckin' dead when the two of you are doing the same shit? Let me run into her and trust when I tell you, I'm going to let her whining ass have it," Mercedes had snapped.

She would get her chance soon. The three of them would have to return to talk with the police, because even though they had closed the case, one of the detectives felt there was more to her murder. It was something that needed to be dealt with, but not tonight

"So Mr. Davis, don't keep me in suspense, enlighten me on your new investment," Dreamer asked.

"We're a little anxious aren't we?" Drew winked. He reached inside his jacket pocket and pulled out an envelope and handed it to her. "Open it," he said.

Intrigue was written over her face. As she read the pages, her eyes began to fill with water, she couldn't believe it. She looked at the papers again, checked the name again, she was now the owner of a $750,000 home in Miami.

"Shut the front door," she kept screaming. Thank goodness Drew had reserved a private room for the two of them. She hadn't stopped screaming. "Are you serious? You're playing a joke on me. OMG!! Drew ahhhh."

Before he could reply, Dream was planting kisses all over his face then suddenly she stopped and sat down. There was a look of concern that covered her face.

"Drew, I have to ask, where did you get this type of money? You paid for this house in cash. What are you doing, please don't tell me you're still in the life, you promised," Dreamer asked with seriousness in her tone.

"Relax gyrl, one question at a time. I told you, the properties I own are doing well as you can see and when I got out of the game I made some smart, sound investments, you can relax, that's why I'm on the property with you. I knew you would be skeptical, but I told you, this time around I know what it takes to win your heart and keep you. Love and honesty are at the top of the list and I promise to give you both. Bae, I know what you've been through and what you're still going through. I also know that everyone is suspect with you right now, but baby I got you, I got us. When I tell you I got you, you got to trust me I got this, for real.

Do you honestly believe that I would destroy my chances of having a future with you or that I would make the same mistakes that drove you to leave me the first time?" he asked.

Drew had thought of everything. He had made arrangements for them to leave one of the docks after they left the restaurant for an afternoon on the water, cruising down the bay.

She had fallen in love with him and there was no denying it, whatever had happened in their past was minuscule to what he was giving to her now. They spent the next four hours out on the beautiful Biscayne Bay and down to Key Biscayne where she fell in love with the lighthouse that sat offshore. Their final destination had been reached, Venetian Island. Dream looked at the home and wondered what they were doing there. It was beautiful to say the least. They stepped of the yacht and headed up the walkway.

"Drew this home is beautiful, are we meeting some of your friends here?" Dreamer asked.

"I hope not," Drew replied and said nothing more.

She looked at him with a puzzled face. Drew had a strange smile on his face, but he was trying to capture the look in her eyes when she realized where they were. She thought to herself, this couldn't possibly be the home he had purchased for her, couldn't be. The Waterfront home was full of luxury. Seven bedrooms, six and a half baths, and over 7600sq ft., polished natural stone floors, ceilings that gave you nights filled with stars and days full of sun rays. The home was lavished throughout with glass 30 feet high and sky terraces that were stunning. It was two stories with 105 degrees of open bay water frontage. It was private and you could feel the serenity when you walked in the sliding glass doors, just breathtaking.

He loved her, if she had questioned his love and sincerity before, it had disappeared. No chance of turning back or walking away now. She loved the home, but she loved him even more. He had come into her life offsetting the upsets and making everything that was wrong, right. No pressure, he had allowed her to handle things at her own pace. He had filled her void, the hole that was in her heart.

She began to cry, it had been a long road and she never could have imagined a love like the one she was experiencing with Drew. "He loves me," she thought to herself, "Drew really loves me." And this was true, he always had. So when they finally made love that night in their new home, it had sealed what they had both longed for and wanted to say to one another.

"Dream, I love you," Drew said.

"And I love you more," she replied.

Never in all her years, did she believe that she would find a love like the one she shared with Drew. She found herself thinking about him at the most inopportune times or touching herself wishing that he was near. She never got enough of being with him.

Years may have separated them, but it had not stolen their love and passion for one another. That night they made love until they were exhausted with each other, making up for lost love and time had proved to be the best. The love they shared for one another completed each other, everything about it was right. Drew had taken her from a past that had devastated her world and shook her foundation, showed her what they could share in the present and what he was willing to share with her in the future.

"I don't ever want you to feel any pressure and I definitely don't want you to rush into anything that you're not comfortable with. I've always had love for you and you know that, but now I can show you better than tell you. We're not new to each other Dream, remember time was the only thing between us, oh yeah, I can't forget your marriage, but I would have waited that out too, because eventually, it would have turned out just like it has. Look ma, when I say that I won't lose you again, I mean it. I'm not going to lose you, it's not an option. The house is yours, ours, but I bought it for you and I want you to enjoy it," Drew said.

Dream's eyes began to water, she knew that Drew was genuine about his gift, all of them, his feelings and love for her were sincere. She would have never imagined their paths would have crossed again. Next to Mercedes, he had become her rock, and he had definitely made her happy.

She didn't believe she could love anyone else after Patience, but Drew was proving her wrong. "All things in moderation and all things when you walk by faith in God," she told herself. They had seen each other at their worst and their best, she could depend on him. Things were slowly starting to feel like normal, and it felt good.

**SECOND CHANCES…**

Dreamer felt the warmth of Drew's body next to hers; she snuggled into his arms and felt him pull her closer. She loved waking up next to him, their life together made her feel complete. It appeared that Drew had given her the world and she had never been as happy as she was at that moment.

"Good morning beautiful," he whispered into her ear and kissed her lightly.

"Good morning to you," she replied.

Last night had been something they would treasure for years to come. From the first kiss they shared after touring the house, to one of the bedroom's that faced the beach, the mixture of warmth and coolness that came from the house and ocean surrounded their bodies. Their chemistry was undeniable and their love for one another was priceless. The warmth of Drew's breath on her ear sent chills through her body, intensifying her need to feel him closer to her. The gentle kisses he planted on her neck and her back had her breathing heavy. She loved him and she didn't have to say a word, he knew it when he looked into her eyes.

Pandora's Box had been opened and a floodgate of memories and feelings evolved.

"What's on your mind love?" Drew asked.

"Honestly, being here with you like this…all the time. Drew I love our home and I love you," Dream said.

"Excuse me, can you say that again," Drew asked with a slight laugh.

"I love being here with you?" she said.

'No, not that," he smiled.

"I love our home," she said.

"You're getting closer," he winked.

"Oh, I love you," Dreamer said as she turned to face him.

He pulled her close and before she knew it, she had straddled his love again, repeating the journey they had taken not long ago. She smiled, this was the happiest she had been in what seemed as though a lifetime

"Hey," he said.

"Hey yourself," she replied.

"Heard you have a date tonight," Drew teased.

"He's some kind of special. Did you hear he just bought us the most beautiful home on Venetian Island? Yeah, he's a keeper, she laughed. "But I'm not to sure if he's still going to be crazy about me, because we need to shower and leave our stunning home because I have a meeting in a couple of hours that I can't miss with some very important clients today," Dreamer said.

"I don't think he'll be that upset if you let him join you," Drew smiled.

"Oh really," she said.

"Really," as he kissed her lightly.

It was an hour later before they stepped out of the shower. Drew knew Dreamer was good for running late so he had Mercedes call and reschedule the times of her appointments. Dream was always amazed with the way Drew would think of everything. There used to be a time when she would compare him to Patience, but Drew was incomparable, he was the man hands down. When her world was falling apart, he stepped in and stepped up to handle what she couldn't and then some.

Her homes were filled with his touch and every detail was given significant thought, he had put his heart and soul into making and keeping her happy. He had taken her away when her heart was broken, devastated and confused, when she had lost Diamond and her soon to be ex-husband was charged with her murder. There was no doubt that he had stood by her and he loved her. This time around, their second chance, he was determined to do it right, leaving no stone unturned and nothing up to chance.

Drew had to laugh a little as he thought about her while they were getting dressed. Dream had put in the work, baby gyrl had worked hard and she reaped the rewards and benefits that came with it. She deserved to be loved unconditionally and not just in the sense of the word. He remembered and knew her heart; something he was glad to find had not hardened in the mist of all that had gone wrong. He vowed to treat it with love and care. She had just shared a part of herself with him and he respected her and wanted her to be comfortable in her own time, he wasn't going anywhere and he needed her to be secure in that, there was no pressure, he would have waited.

Their closets were his and her walk-ins and she came out stunning. She wore a pair of Black Manolo Blahnik Zimrino leather slingback pumps and a black and white polka dot wraparound dress that accented her figure, very flattering and appropriate for meeting with her clients at Azul.

Azul was an upscale restaurant that sat on Briskell Key Drive. Reservations came highly recommended and Dream had taken the liberty of doing so weeks ago. She had sat her business strategy aside for a moment and entertained the thoughts of the night she had just spent with Drew, she wanted to turn around and do it all over again, but she knew there was not time for that, this meeting was important.

Business had been good to her and was looking up. Darryl had kept his word and plugged her company in some of the ventures he was taking on and in return she had produced. His clients were impressed with her skills and now they were hers as well. Darryl and Dream had kept in touch outside of business since their meeting in Philly and their reconnection had been a good one.

Her meeting with Damon Lassiter had gone well also. Dream had pitched him her presentation on her upcoming Non-Profit Organization, *A Father, A Friend*, an organization she had came up with years ago, but never moved on it. The organization would cater to single fathers who were supporting and raising their child/ren on their own and Dream felt they went unrecognized. The non-profit would recognize several fathers each month and honor them in a breakfast, luncheon or a dinner. They would offer workshops for fathers to interact and voice their concerns on raising a child as a single parent into today's society. At the end of the year there would be a Black and White affair held honoring them. Lassiter liked what he heard and was glad to come aboard and support the project as well as invest behind it while bringing on several other investors.

By the close of the meeting Dreamer was on cloud nine. She had closed two deals this trip. The driver met her outside of Azul's and took her back to Venetian Island. Her ride back was not only consumed with the deal she had just successfully closed, but Drew. He had given her the best of everything. Her cell ranged, it was Mercedes.

"How you livin' mami?" she asked. Mercedes had checked them out of their hotel room and was going to meet her at the house.

"Your gyrl can't complain. I closed the deal! They accepted my proposal and Lassiter brought on several other investors. Can this day get any better?" Dream yelled.

"That's what up Ma. So I guess you're not upset with me anymore?" Mercedes asked.

"Right now, we're good. I'll get you on one of my bad days and you know I will have one," Dream laughed.

She had to admit this was the happiest she had been in months and the trip to Miami had turned into more than she could have ever imagined. Drew had given her more than a summer home there or helped built her dream home in Tampa, he had given her his heart and love and she had finally opened the door to share hers with him.

She still found it hard to believe, she had a luxurious home she was going to hate too leave, but of course she would come back as often as she could. Now the matter at hand was flying to Barbados in a couple of weeks to meet with detectives who were still investigating Diamond's murder and trying to figure out how to keep Mercedes from killing Shay while they were there.

The two hadn't spoke since the funeral where Mercedes lost it on her. Dream had spoke to her a few times, lately, but hadn't mentioned it to Mercedes for fear she would go ballistic and she was going to have too deal with that soon enough.

Mercedes was in the kitchen when Dream walked in scaling through the Sub-Zero refrigerator which was filled with everything one could imagine. Mercedes grabbed a bottle of Krug Reims Champagne, an $1100 bottle. Dream grabbed a couple of glasses and they went into the living room. A beautiful white sofa faced the ocean view through the ceiling to floor glass sliding doors. Dream pulled the doors open and a breeze came in off the water, it filled the room with the scent of saltwater and the warmth of jasmine, she had lingering in the air. She loved her new home and all that came with it.

"So what's up gyrl?" Mercedes asked.

"Still taking all of this in, it's a little overwhelming. Can you believe this? I just had a house built, haven't got comfortable in it yet and now this?" Dream beamed.

"Enjoy your new home and happiness," Mercedes said as she poured them a glass of champagne.

"It's beautiful. I could put my house in here and still have more than enough room to enjoy," Dream smiled.

"What's on your mind, real talk? You've been my gyrl forever and something's bothering you." Mercedes asked.

"I'm in love with Drew," Dream blushed.

"Not a problem. It's about damn time. I really thought you were going to fuck this up for me, for sure," Mercedes laughed.

"Come again," Dream smiled at her friend.

"**Real Talk**: Like I said, it's about damn time. How long have we've known each other? A lifetime, we've walked some tough roads together, good and bad times. I watched you step away from the game, build your own business, married and divorced an asshole and you've survived it all. I've stayed up late nights, cried with you and watched you cry and woke up and we did it all over again. You're the only sister I have and I love you. I know what this is about and it's time to let Patience go ma. You've done all that you can do, it's over. You've filed for the divorce, sign the papers and let that be your closure. You can't fix what is damaged, and Dream, it's damaged.

I have to commend Drew. He has kept his word, no pressure. The man hasn't left your side. He has given you a small piece of the world since he has been back in your life, he has your back and I believe that, he shows it in everything he does. To love once is special, to have it present itself a second time, is to embrace it for a lifetime.

When you think about Patience, think about if he would have told the truth once, your marriage wouldn't be damaged and it wouldn't be in the hands of a judge.

This is the happiest I have seen you in months. You're relaxed, smiling and that's what's up. Allow this man to love you. When he called me and asked if I could get you away for a week, I told him no problem, no questions asked. And once he filled me in and showed me online the house he had purchased for you, hell I asked him if it had a room for me because I wanted to move in.

He's unbelievable Dream, he loves you and your happiness is all that matters to him. I couldn't be happier for you, look at this place, it's amazing not to mention the home he just finished for you. Enjoy the moment. Live, love and laugh as Van would say. Life is to short, Carpe Diem, because in the blink of an eye, it could be gone.

Look at what happened to Diamond, she was at the top of her game and some bullshit took her out. When that man comes in tonight, give him the cookies and toss that shit up," Mercedes said as she picked up her glass and tilted a toast. She took a sip and continued.

"Don't let your past keep you from your future Mami," she said.

"I'm there with you," Dream said.

"Then it's settled. Damn! Look at the time, we're on a flight back to Tampa in the morning, so I'll say goodnight because I think I hear your man coming through the door. See you, in the morning. And I take it you will be hitting the bed or somewhere soon," Mercedes snickered. "Love ya."

Dream sat on the deck with her glass of champagne, listening to the tides roll to shore. Drew had picked the perfect home for them. It was private, no neighbors, he knew how she hated that and it was on the water. She loved the ocean always had even as a child. The night was warm and the air was still thick, the sky was filled with stars and she could see a couple of Yacht's out on the water, but she didn't have to worry about them docking near them.

She breathed in the saltwater air, laid her head back and took in the sky. She thought about how happy Drew had truly made her. Not just the material things he had given her, but what he had given her of himself, his love, it was priceless.

She didn't hear him as he stepped out on the deck, but felt his arms around her waist. She rested her head back on his chest and took in his scent, tonight he wore Versace. His cologne lingered in the air. He kissed the side of her neck and asked her how her day had gone. She shared all of her wonderful news with him and he was happy for her. He was smiling.

"What's with the smile? Not that I ever get tired of seeing those dimples of yours," she asked.

"I'm glad to see your smiling. I know how rough these last couple of years, have been for you," he said.

"Thanks to you and Mercedes," she said. Dream didn't realize that the entire time she was talking Drew had begun to loosen her dress.

"Hey beautiful," he whispered.

"Hey yourself, you could have warned me," she replied.

"Baby your good," he dropped his keys on the table. "You guys had a party without me I see."

"No party, just a small bite to eat and a few drinks," Dreamer whispered.

"What's the occasion, especially if you've had a drink," Drew asked.

"I'm celebrating, haven't you heard? I have a new man in my life and I'm loving him." Dream let out a faint moan.

"Anybody I know," Drew teased.

"I think you might, he's close to you."

"How close," Drew asked.

"Seems like he's a little closer to me," Dream said.

"Want him closer," he asked.

"Please," she purred.

Drew's love was unbelievable. Dreamer was lightweight inebriated and it was definitely heightening the sexual ride she was about to take. She loved how gentle Drew was with her, his hands caressed her body as his mouth covered her breast and aroused her nipples. She moaned again in pleasure as he unsnapped her bra and dropped her dress to the deck.

She could feel his love pressing up again her. Dreamer looked into his eyes as she unbuttoned his shirt and placed wet kisses on his chest. She loved the way he smelled.

Drew looked down into her eyes and saw everything there that he loved about her, second chances, he thought to himself. He kissed her lips and held her like he was afraid to let her go, that if he did she wouldn't return. It was intoxicating.

The breeze had picked up and the waves were hitting the shore with some roughness. The moon was full and the sky was filled with stars. Drew sat Dreamer down and the warmth of his mouth caressed her enter thigh as he took in her sweet scent. His tongue took a slow glide towards her moistness and he entered her with gentle kisses, wet licks and sucks. Her body shook as she moaned uncontrollably. Each time Drew went deeper, with her hands around his head, pulling him closer to her, she gyrated, her hips in the pleasure he was giving her. Three, four, five mini orgasms back to back they continued to come, he was making her weak. He led her from the deck to the white sanded beach, they believed in taking risk. Drew took her in his arms and kissed her with such passion it made her legs weak. Their bodies disturbed the sand as they became one. He filled her with his love and she accepted all of him. The motion of their bodies moving to a seductive, intoxicating rhythm underneath a moonlit sky filled with stars, the unspoken words between the two was golden.

With each thrust, Drew entered her moist walls and he felt like heaven inside of her, their bodies were one. Dreamer's legs wrapped around his body, her arms around his neck taking him in deeper, she gasped for air as she accepted all of him, not wanting the night to ever end. He took control of her body with every stroke, seven, eight, nine, they wouldn't stop she didn't want them to. Ten, eleven, twelve, "Oh my God," he heard her whispers, "Don't stop, Drew don't...stop," she could barely speak. She looked up into his eyes and she knew, this was where she always wanted to be and he felt the same.

In that moment they shared a night of memories, old and new, unforgettable. It had been two years that Drew had waited for Dreamer, on her terms, no pressure she had finally became one with him and he wasn't going anywhere.

"I got you," Drew whispered.

"You got me?" she asked.

"Forever," he replied.

She moved in closer to him as he held her in his arms. Dreamer had fallen in love with Drew and he had done the same with her. Loving her and keeping her happy was going to be easy, getting her to say yes to his marriage proposal was going to be something different.

The morning came fast. Dreamer hated the idea of having to leave her new home, not to mention having to get out of bed. Drew was already up and showered and smiling at her when she woke up.

"I got your cookies," he laughed.

"You're childish," she smiled.

"That's not what you were saying earlier," he smacked her on her ass.

"You got me there," Dreamer said.

"No, I got you out there and there," he winked at her. "Hey you want something to eat before we get out of here?"

"Cranberry juice baby, please," she replied as she walked into the bathroom.

"That's it?" he asked.

She had stepped in the shower. Drew hit the kitchen where he found Mercedes nursing a Mimosa.

"So you polished off my $1100 bottle of champagne?" Drew teased.

"I finished a couple of bottles, this one's for the road. You know we're off to Barbados next week and I have to be armed and ready for whatever," Mercedes said.

"Yeah, I'm moving some things around so I can fly down with you guys. Have you talked to Shay?" Drew asked.

"That's what I'm getting ready for, another drink should take care that. I have to prepare myself for that bitch. Haven't seen her since the funeral, don't know what my reaction or my reflexes are going to be," Mercedes said.

"You guys need to work that out. You're supposed to be best friends," Drew said.

"My besties in there, and anyway that tricks not telling the truth and until she does, Houston we have a problem. Changing the subject, thank you," Mercedes said.

"For what," Drew asked.

"For bringing some joy into my gyrl's life, this has been the happiest I've seen her in months. Listen, Dream is the only sister I have, get where I'm coming from?" Mercedes said.

"I hear you and you don't have to worry, I got her," Drew said, assurance in his voice.

"Looks serious, what I miss?" Dreamer asked as she walked into the kitchen.

"I was just threatening Drew," Mercedes said.

"She scares me. Hey bae, are your things ready to go out to the car?" Drew asked.

"I pulled everything to the door, we're good," Dream replied.

Dream really hated the idea of leaving her new home. She was looking for any excuse to get back to Venetian Islands and no reason at all was winning. She knew she would need a few weeks to recoup after their trip to Barbados, so she would run it by Drew and see if he could get away for a month or so. She was sure Mercedes would join her if Drew couldn't spend the entire month. She took one last look around her new home and it held some special memories for her.

The driver was waiting out front for them after loading the car. The ride to the airport Drew made a few calls. Their driver had been instructed to take them to Miami International Airport, but not to their departure gate, but to a private Aircraft Hangar. Mercedes and Dreamer looked at each other confused.

"Drew baby where are we going?" Dream asked.

"Home," he smiled.

"Yeah, but our flight is leaving from the opposite direction," she replied.

"No, we're going the right way," he said.

"Look the two of you, just get me on the damn plane, I have a terrible headache and I think I'm about to get sick, so if the two of you are about to argue, can you do it on the plane and do it quietly?" Mercedes interrupted.

The driver pulled into the hangar where he stopped and unloaded their bags and opened their doors.

"Whose plane is this Drew?" Dreamer quizzed.

"Don't panic, it's not mine. I just wanted some privacy and I thought we all could use it. Every now and then when I have business that requires some last minute travel and I don't have time for book a flight, I'll go through a friend who will let me use his company plane to handle my business. I didn't burn all my bridges along the way," Drew said.

While he was explaining things to her, Mercedes had stumbled on the plane. Dream's mind was racing a mile a minute. "Not after this week Drew, or last night. Not after I told you I loved you," she thought to herself.

She couldn't go down this road again, not with what she had been through with Patience. "Please God, don't let Drew still be in the game, I just walked away from this hell," she said.

When their plane reached Tampa International Airport and pulled into the aircraft hangar things were solemn. Dreamer hadn't said a word the entire flight and Mercedes had slept which was a good thing because Dream couldn't handle her right now. Drew had tried talking to Dream but she shut that down. There was something he wasn't telling her and until he did, silence was what he was working with.

It had been almost two weeks and Dream had not spoken to Drew. Not from his lack of trying, she just refused to accept his phone calls and he didn't want to pressure her so he stayed at his apartment, to give her some time to calm down.

He knew what she had gone thru and she couldn't believe he would do this to her. Her cell ranged, it was Drew again and unless he was ready to explain what the hell was going on he could stay unanswered. As she ignored the call, he walked through the front door.

Damn, after two weeks of not seeing him he looked good and smelled good. He was a sight for sore eyes and was wearing Usher's, Untouchable, damn.

"It's like that between us?" Drew asked.

Dreamer didn't respond.

"I told you and gave you my word I'm done with the streets. Dream damn, has that nigga hurt you that bad that you don't know what's real anymore? Listen, I do well for myself, damn well as you can see, I haven't come this far to be stupid. You said you trusted me. I'm not your past Dream, not the one who destroyed you faith in people or broke your heart. You walked away from the game and me because you were ready. I still had some work to put in and that's what I did, I'm not apologizing for that. And I won't let you hold me accountable for what some other man has done. I love you and I'm not going anywhere, but you're gonna have to trust me," Drew said.

"Are you finished?" Dreamer asked.

"Nall, I'm just getting started. Either you love me or you don't. I've been keeping things real with you since we hooked back up, don't flake out on me now and say that you don't know me," Drew continued. "I didn't fuck you over!"

"Excuse you, I thought I knew Patience," Dreamer snapped.

"Yeah, that's your problem, I'm NOT Patience. I've been nothing but sympathetic to all that you've been through, but you can't hold his indiscretions and his downfalls against me. I wasn't the one who did those things to you. Baby, I need you to let it go, or we don't stand a chance. I'm competing with a man whose not here. I've respected your space and your boundaries I've stepped back and applied no pressure whatsoever. I've respected you and understood, even when I didn't, I knew that you needed time to heal, I ain't that guy that crushed your world and rocked your foundation ma. I'm the man that's in love with you and trying like hell to get you to see that," Drew said.

"I love you too," Dreamer finally said.

"Than if you mean that, roll with me, not against me. I got you. And Dream, I love you more, that's why I want you to marry me."

"Ok, so now you've got jokes?" Dream said, not taking him serious.

"I'm not joking or laughing," Drew replied as he pulled out a medium sized black box with a silver ribbon around it.

Dream stared in disbelief, speechless. Words didn't come any faster when Drew opened the box and revealed a four carat Titanium diamond ring in the most unbelievable setting. And the tears were uncontrollably.

"Drew," was all she could say.

"Dreamer, I'm serious about everything I've said to you and shared with you. I don't need months or years to know that I love you, this right here that we have is what I want all the time," Drew said as he kneeled down and looked up into her brown eyes that told him, she thought she had seen everything. "Dreamer Marie Jones, I love you in ways unimaginable and being without you this time around is not what I want. When I think about the rest of our lives, we're complete in each other together, will marry me?" Drew asked.

"Drew, how do I do this?" Dream asked.

"You say yes. You're not taking a chance here, our love has always stood on its own and it's proven that because here we are again, given a second chance," Drew replied.

"I'm not even out of one marriage to think about another," Dream said.

"But you will be. And when it's all done and said, you will be Mrs. Drew Davis," Drew smiled.

No doubt she loved him and he has been the best thing to happen to her ever. She would be crazy to let him get away. So she gave him the answer that had been in her heart for more than a period of time.

"Yes, Mr. Davis, yes I will marry you," Dreamer screamed.

## MY BIG NEWS…

"OMG! That's what's up," Mercedes hollered. "We're going out. Drew got the cookies and damnnnnn gyrl, they must have been good 'cause the diamonds you're rockin' ma~mi are unbelievably hot," she said.

"Yeah," was all Dreamer could say, still in a state of shock that she had said yes, but she had been hoping that he would ask for a while. Beyond happy was putting it mild she was in a state of awe. Drew had just made her the happiest woman in the world, asking her to share his life with him. She couldn't stop staring at the ring. She loved material things wasn't attached to them, but loved them the same, what woman didn't and her ring was something to go crazy over, but it didn't compare to where it come from, that place was priceless.

"So you guys set a date?' Mercedes asked.

"No, I still have to get divorced remember. You know Patience isn't going to feel this," Dream said.

"Flip him the bird, shit. He can't feel shit no way. His trash, another's treasure, not that your trash boo, but you get where I'm comin' from," Mercedes said.

"He wrote me," Dream said in a whisper.

"So, he writes a lot of damn people," Mercedes replied with raised eyebrows.

"It still hurts and a part of me still loves him. You know, I meet with Chance next week for the final signing," Dreamer said.

"So when's the party? You promised one, remember. And do I detect some kind of sadness in your voice? You just got engaged to a man that adores you. You should be on cloud nine. Hell, you should be feeling some kind of turbulence up there because not only have you gotten engage, given a beautiful home on Venetian Island, but had a home built from the ground up all in two years, that's a lot of love. So what's your problem again? Oh I know, you can't forget dead weight," Mercedes said.

"The end of an era," Dream said.

"See ya! It's about damn time, it's been two years too damn long, let it go already, DAMN! You're beating this dead horse more than Patience. Can you say wrap it up? Let Patience write, call, send currier pigeon, Indian chief, smoke signals if necessary, wrap this shit up and quit procrastinating, move on, we have a wedding to plan," Mercedes grabbed her Fiji water, her purse and keys and stormed out the door.

**MERCEDES...**

Dream and I have been friends forever, the only sister I have and though she has Tori, we're all each other truly have. Tori, is just a fill-in, she exists but doesn't. Bitch has some issues, but that's another story for another time.

We're ride or die besties and we always have each others back. I keep telling you guys that don't I? Especially about our many chapters with Patience and tonight she needed an ear full of get over his tired in jail ass. I've watched him fuck over her for years, but a true friend, such as myself, keeps it real, speaks her piece and our friendship is tighter than ever and has stood the tests of time. Patience has taken high score on fucking my gyrl over in a thousand ways. You know the book, a 1,001 ways to fuck well he has performed them all on Dream. She knows how I feel and I don't talk behind my gyrl's back, but this shit right here is getting out of control. So what he wrote or called. His lying ass is still on the same shit as he was when he was on the streets.

I see a different person in her when she is with Drew, she wears him well. Finally, someone who has her back loves her and has her best interest in heart. Now he wants to marry her, HELL YEAH! I say, that's what's up, but she's concerned about Patience feelings. I say, fuck his feelings. When he was on the streets, he had nothing but chance and opportunity to show her he loved her, but the best his sorry ass could do was cheat on her. Now that his simple ass is on lockdown, he needs her friendship and her strength to get him through his time. Where the hell are Chantel and Shaunnie now? I'm sure not far, but those two bitches are giving him the blues right about now, trust me. Who held Dream down for the past two years while she nursed a broken heart? When she needed her husband, where the hell was Patience? I'll tell you were he was, runnin' up in Shaunnie's ass, interfering in Chantel's life and giving his wife all the mad drama he brought home from the streets, simple ass.

He wasn't around when Van or Diamond died. My bad, the son-of-a-bitch has been charged in her murder and she's concerned about his feelings. A sympathy letter was what he wrote. He wants her to forgive him so that he can free his conscience. The hell with that, it should eat his ass up every time he thinks about her after what he put her through.

I've watched him hurt her time and time again and each time she forgave him, I never understood why. They've had this weird type of relationship from the start. She's been a good one to overlook his "indiscretions" as she calls them. I'll call it what it is, bullshit.

Patience is a loser, a fuck up at his best. Shaunnie and Chantel, those two nothings deserve him, not my gyrl. Let him continue to roll with his gyrl Shaunnie, that's who he wanted, let that be the reason to say fuck him, even more.

She just brought a home, her business is doing better than ever, Drew just dropped some mad paper on her a summer/winter home, not to mention the rock he put on her finger. If she fucks this up, our friendship is on the line for sure, I promise I will have her committed.

Dream's my bestie and her being happy means a lot to me, she's hurt enough, it's time to live, love and laugh. She knows I'm pissed because in all of our years, we haven't had an argument. We agree to disagree and respect each others space, arguing is not what we do. I'll get at her later.

## DREAMER...

After Mercedes left I called Chance and moved up our appointment for me to sign my divorce papers, there was no need to prolong the inevitable. Patience wasn't coming home anytime soon and our marriage over. Most of all, he wasn't checkin' for me.

I had received several letters from him and knew it came as a surprise when I replied, it surprised me as well. I had sat down and read his letters over and over again looking for something that would help me understand how we ended up here, but no matter how many times I read them, there was no answer. He had destroyed our home and threw our marriage to the wind.

He professed his love, said he was sorry, said I would never understand his reasons for the hurt he caused me...and he was right, I would never understand. It's taken two years to heal my broken heart and Drew has been here every step of the way. Through Van and Diamond's deaths, he's held my hand, wiped my tears and stood beside me and now he's about to take this trip with me again to Barbados to talk with the investigators about Diamond's murder. I couldn't ask for a better man. I feel truly blessed having him in my life I couldn't love him anymore than I do at this very moment.

More than anything, I understand Mercedes frustration. She's seen me through a lot of what Patience has put me through and it's been pure hell. She's the sister I don't have in Tori and I couldn't ask for a better one, so I understand how emotional this is for her, hell it's emotional for me, but she's a ride or die sister-friend and I'm glad she's in my corner.

There's so much going on in my life lately and in the mist of it all I'm getting married. I can't believe I'm going to do it again, but this time I have it all in Drew. Life is a funny thing sometimes, if we could just wait and be a little patient, happiness would not pass us by. Just stand still and let God. He knows exactly what He's doing and what's good for us, we just have to trust in Him and in His time, not ours. He doesn't need our help.

There has been so much on my mind, the divorce, the engagement, two new homes, falling in love with an unbelievable man and the fact that Patience has been on my mind a little more than usual. I received my divorce papers and I decided to sit and write Patience. What will I say? How will I tell him that Drew and I are getting married? Why do I feel as though I need to tell him anything?

So I wrote him, told him I filed for the divorce and that my lawyer would be contacting him. Told him that I was finally giving him what he had been asking for, now we both could move on with our lives. You know he sent my letter back. Told me I didn't give him shit and please don't ever write him again. Damn, it's like that? I thought he would be glad to share the big news with Shaunnie. I had given him what he had been asking for, his freedom from me, to be with her and his son as a family.

I wanted to reply, but I didn't. Once again I would respect his wishes. It's sad that our lives had come to this. Chance contacted me a few weeks later, we had a scheduled court date it was a finalization on what had become the end.

Not only was I dealing with a upcoming divorce, I wanted to make some time to talk to Shay, we were less than a week away from flying back to Barbados. Shay and I had only spoke a couple of times briefly since Diamond's funeral and I wanted to give her some time to grieve and deal with her loss as well. So I decided to call her and see if we could meet up for lunch.

"Hey Shay, it's Dream, got a minute?'

"Hey," she replied quietly. She hadn't been herself since Diamond's death. She had been dealing with a lot since then. Her husband had taken the kids and moved out and she had lost a little business at the salons once people had found out what had gone down with Diamond. Gossip was hurting her business and it seemed as though she couldn't get a handle on things.

"So what's up gyrl, I was calling to see if you were ready? I was on my way," Dream said.

"I'm on my way out now, see you there," Shay said.

"Cool, see you in a minute," Dream replied.

Shay looked good, considering all that had gone on. She sported a fresh new cut, with a hit of color, she wore it well. She was wearing a white floor length dress with a black belt, she looked relaxed.

I was driving Mercedes, Rover Onyx and was blasting Ledesi's new CD. I loved her truck and hated giving it back whenever I borrowed it.

We pulled up at the same time and the valet parked our vehicals. We shared a awkward hug and walked in silence. Honestly, I didn't know what to say, it was one of those strained moments. But Shay broke the ice.

"I hear congratulations are in order," she said.

"Thanks and yes, I'm excited. Drew is a blessing," I said.

"So have you guys set a date?" Shay asked.

"Diamond's birthday," I said.

There was that awkward silence again. I could tell that it took Shay by surprise. She held a far away look in her eyes and then the tears came.

"You want to talk about it?" I asked.

Shay shook her head, excused herself from the table and headed towards the bathroom. We had decided to have lunch in the Don Ceasar hotel it was convenient for me because I had business in town. When Shay returned the waiter took our order and we sat in silence, for what appeared to be the longest time. I thought to myself how ridicules we were being, we had all been friends and we shared in the same loss.

"Shay, what happened?" I asked.

"I don't know what you mean," she replied.

Thank God Mercedes wasn't with us, Shay had just opened a door to whip ass. Her response would have definitely got her a beat down.

"You know what I'm talking about, it's been almost two years and you haven't said a word about any of this, and I need some answers. Diamond was my friend too. She was my bestie too, remember? How can you sit there and tell me with a clear conscience that you don't know what was going on with her?" I said.

"She wasn't who you thought she was," Shay whispered. "She could be a real bitch at times and brass to say the least. She knew what we were into could get us killed, but she was all about the money, always about the money. Now I have to worry about whether her unfinished business could end my life as well. Diamond got careless. I sacrificed my marriage, my kids, my business because I trusted my friend and I use the word loosely. I've damn near lost it all thanks to her," Shay said.

Dreamer looked a little surprised to hear Shay speak of her gyrl that way. They were close, right?

"Help me understand how two intelligent women such as yourselves, got caught up in some shit like this and how does Diamond end up dead?" I asked.

"I don't know what went wrong. She was supposed to call me and she never did. I kept calling her phone and it was going to voicemail, she and Keyon had been fighting for weeks so I figured it was just another one of those nights. They had left together and I don't know what went wrong," Shay snapped.

Dream looked at Shay sympathetically for a moment then it turned into a look that could throw knives. Could she possibly be trying to play the victim in all of this? Dream counted herself down before she spoke.

"Listen Shay, I'm not your enemy here. I'm trying to understand what happened to Diamond, trying to find closure in a fucked up situation and nothings making sense. I thought we were on the same page. I'm sorry if your feeling interrogated, but it is what it is. And today, right here, right now, either your friend or foe, and I stand firmly by my words," I said.

"I'm under a lot of stress. The police are riding me, the husband has moved out and taken the kids and he's damn near kept me from seeing them, hell we're on the verge of a divorce and I am trying my best to hold shit together, so you will have to excuse me if I can not entertain you and your suspicions. My businesses are suffering and I am trying to keep them above water with all the gossip that's floating around. So if my answers are short, curt and un-appeasing to your snooping ass alter-ego, so be it. And I stand by my words," Shay said.

Shay was just one word away from the ass kicking Mercedes had been dying to give her, only she would have to wait in line because Dream was front and center.

"Listen touch sensitive, we could do this all day, but sooner or later the truth is going to come out. Either you can talk to me or the detectives when we get to Barbados, makes me none, I'm sure they're going to be less than nice, so Ms. Smart Ass take your pick," Dreamer said.

"How about I'll talk to neither of you?" Shay replied.

This wasn't the way their luncheon was supposed to go. Maybe Dreamer should have included Mercedes, but it was against her better judgment in order to avoid the drama she was getting now.

"Shay, hold on, I'm not trying to make your life more complicated, I'm just looking for answers that I believe you have. Diamond's death has been tragic for all of us, we need closure and answers, not altercations," Dreamer said.

Maybe if she took another approach, she would get a better response. That would be a NO!

"Listen Dream, just let it go," Shay said.

And surprisingly to her, that's exactly what she did. The waiter bought them the desert menu, Dream asked if she could have hers to go. She excused herself and headed for the restroom. On her way back the waiter met her with her bag and credit card, she left without saying goodbye to Shay. There was nothing else to say.

The relationship between Mercedes, Shay and Dream was all bad. Diamond's death had weighed on them all. They each had to admit their friendship would never be the same. Mercedes and Dream believed Shay knew more than she was telling and that she had a hand in Diamond's murder. Shay felt they were ganging up on her and unsympathetic to her losses.

Dream didn't know what to take away from her lunch with Shay. She wasn't sure if she was scared or if she was just being the bitch she truly could be, but what she knew for sure was that the pressure was getting to her and sooner than later she was sure to slip.

Dream decided to tell Mercedes about their luncheon, she knew she was going to snap, but her intentions of meeting with Shay were good until the bitch fell off the ride. Dream also knew that their flight to Barbados was going to be unbearable and she wasn't sure if Shay was going to back out since she was so defensive at lunch in sharing what she knew.

Dream needed a different approach. She had a few favors she could call in so she decided to have Shay tailed, maybe she would get some of the answers if not all. It would also buy her a little time with Mercedes on the ass whippin' she was sure to put on Shay after she heard how lunch had went.

"Hey," Dream said.

"What's up ma?" Mercedes replied.

"Need you to meet me at the house, say in about an hour," Dream said.

"Sounds important, what gives?" Mercedes asked.

"Tell you when you get here. One hour," Dream hung up.

"Hey love," Dreamer said.

"Hey, beautiful what's up," Drew asked.

"Didn't want you to forget that we're flying out tomorrow," Dream said.

"I'm glad you called, thanks for the heads up, I haven't forgot. I'll get up with you later, it's been a busy day and I still got hours of work left to do before we get out of here," Drew said.

"Couldn't be any worse than mine, but that will hold," she replied.

'What's up, you wanna talk about it?" Drew asked.

"Talk to you later, it's nothing that can't wait. Just needed to drop that bug in your ear," she said.

"Let me wrap some things up and I'll see you in a few hours," he said.

"Ok, later baby," Dream replied.

Her other line was ringing, it was Shay. She let it go to voicemail.

**BARBADOS….**

Grantley Adams International Airport was bittersweet. This wasn't a trip of pleasure and relaxation, Wukking Up was going to have to wait. Mercedes had chosen to sit as far away from Shay as possible, in order to keep the drama down. So far it was working. Our early morning flight was surprisingly quiet and the day was picture perfect.

Drew had put off some work in order to make the trip so he spent a little time catching up on the flight over. Work was the last thing on my mind. Close to landing I began to get nauseous, I guess it was just the idea of being back there and knowing what we were here for. My last trip played over in my head, as though it was yesterday, going to the morgue and having to identify Diamond's body. The feeling of sickness wouldn't let me go and I was boiling over with anger. My luncheon with Shay was pointless. She still refused to talk and I was thinking about letting Mercedes tap that ass to make her cough up the truth, but I knew that wasn't the answer. For a moment, I felt the old me resurface and it scared me, because she wasn't anything nice.

I needed to regain focus. Since this tragedy happened, I've kept in contact with the lead homicide detective on the case. He knew how important it was for me to find out what really happened to my gyrl. He informed me that he had some new leads and that he had some news that might help me understand the real reason Diamond had come to Barbados. We still had no leads on Keyon and his disappearance, but he was the least of my worries. Maybe I should have been concerned, maybe I should have started with him, he possibly could have answered some of my questions.

There was still so much speculation surrounding Diamond's death that I was beginning to believe we would never find out the truth. As much as my trip to Barbados was about Diamond I knew I would need some time to process it all. So before I committed myself completely, I decided on a change of plans for the evening. For the next two weeks we would be on the south coast of Barbados, the St. Lawrence Beach Condominiums. From the rooftop there was a stunning view of the aqua Caribbean Sea. St Lawrence was one of the most beautiful places to stay on the island.

The Tiffany bedroom was my favorite, it reminded me of my home in Miami, the one Drew had just purchased. We were fifteen miles away from the airport and Drew was a little leery about the distance just in case Mercedes needed a quick get away after having to choke Shay out. Finally, the thought of something that made me laugh. The four of us had been the best of friends, there was such a void there without Diamond. We had agreed to meet with the detectives in a couple of days he didn't want to overwhelm us with his findings. So tonight the four of us would meet up at Joset's in St. Lawrence Gap.

It was a beautiful place to get married, Dream thought to herself as she stood on the patio overlooking the body of water. How couldn't she think of her upcoming wedding surrounded by so much beauty? Diamond loved beautiful, elaborate things as well. The last time they had all been there and laughed together was when they ported here during their cruise. She missed her friend.

"Hey beautiful, penny for your thoughts," the warmth of Drew's voice rested on her ear.

Dream turned towards her future husband and felt like the luckiest woman in the world. He embraced her in his arms as she lifted her head to kiss him.

"I was thinking, how did our lives get so off track? We use to look out for one another have each others back. Mercedes is angry and I don't blame her, Shay is defensive and I'm all messed up. Diamond's really gone. Here it is two years later and I haven't gotten over the lost of my best friend. It's starting to sink in and I feel like we're not any closer today than we were when we got the phone call," Dream said.

Drew knew her heart was breaking and he didn't know how to heal it, he just gave her space to find her way and provided a listening ear when she needed to talk. The three of them had tried to repair their friendship after Diamond's death, but they knew it would never be the same. Diamond and Dreamer's relationship had never fully healed after she and Patience were married. After Diamond's reaction and her coldness Dream found it hard to trust her or even call her a friend. Diamond had threw Dream under the bus more than a few times after she learned of the marriage. Thinking about those things didn't help to ease the pain. They were never able to get the trust back after it was broken.

"Maybe when we meet with the detectives tomorrow, you'll have some closure on all of this. I didn't expect this trip to be easy for you, I expected it to do just as it has, open up old wounds and allow you room to heal you've got to believe that. Where's my fighter at? You tired? I got you baby, so go head, get tired, if that's what you need to do. Know this, I got you," Drew said.

"I know that you don't want to here this, but the hardest part of all of this is over. Finding out will only heal your pain. As much as I want to ease your mind and pain, I know I can't, but I'm here if you break," Drew said.

Dream loved Drew and he saw it in her eyes every time she looked at him. Drew was her comfort zone and she was glad that he had come alone. He made her feel secure.

"I love you," she told him.

"Love you more," Drew said.

Mercedes busted up the tender moment the two were sharing.

"Hey you two," she said.

"I'm going to leave you two alone for a while, behave," Drew told Dream and Mercedes.

They both gave him a look.

"So you think Shay is gonna show up?" Mercedes asked.

"I don't know what to expect from her. The way she flipped on me at lunch makes me think she has some head issues," Dream replied.

"When did you have lunch with that hoe? I'll get with you on that, speaking of nuts cases, pull out your license, speak of the devil herself, she walking up," Mercedes smirked.

"Hey," Shay said.

"We weren't sure if you were gonna join us," Dreamer said.

"It wouldn't hurt to get a breath of fresh air and a bite to eat. I've just been overwhelmed I have a lot on my plate. I didn't mean to snap on you at lunch the other day. I was served divorce papers and I really couldn't handle anything else," Shay said.

"Ummm," Mercedes said.

"Shay, I'm sorry. How are the kids handling this?" Dream asked.

"He won't let me see or talk to them. When this whole mess started out I couldn't be alone with them, now I have nothing. We agreed to tell them when I get back. He's taken my babies from me," Shay said.

"You took them from you, you selfish bitch," Mercedes whispered.

She had promised to be on her best behavior tonight. Good luck on that one. They all knew how hard that was going to be. Dream was hoping they would at least make it through dinner.

Drew broke the moment that was slowly brewing. He joined them on the patio and motioned them towards their table. Once they were seated, the night turned out better than any of them could have expected. Mercedes kept her word and held down the smart remarks and the snappy comments. No arguments brewed and Dream was thankful for that.

After dinner was over Drew and Dream excused themselves.

"Yo cookies got you a villa the last time mami and a marriage proposal, don't come back with a baby this time," Mercedes joked.

"That will be a NO Alex," Dream winked.

Drew was not amused.

"Oh, so now you know Alex?" Mercedes laughed.

Mercedes and Shay were left alone, against Dream's better judgment. She wasn't sure if it was the best thing to do, but it was something they were going to have to fix on their own.

Mercedes sat, waiting on Shay to say anything, just hoping it wasn't something to get her ass kicked.

"It's beautiful here," Shay finally said.

Mercedes didn't respond. The two hadn't spoke since Diamond's funeral and speaking was pushing it. Mercedes had lost it on Shay on the flight back after identifying Diamond's body; she lost it on her again at the funeral.

"You knew she was in trouble and you didn't say a word. Diamond wasn't just getting her ass kicked by Keyon, she had some real players looking for her and you knew that. What does that say about you as a friend? Who does that? Wait a minute…you did," Mercedes said.

"Can we try and not do this tonight?" Shay asked.

"No, let's, there's no better time than the present. Dream might be ok with you brushing this off and backing down, but you know that's not the case with me and I'm not trying to hear it," Mercedes said calmly. Mercedes saw her words had put a bit of fear in Shay. Once Mercedes was calm, you never knew what the hell to expect. Shay was uneasy, she thought before she spoke.

"Mercedes listen, Diamond was complicated. I was as close to her as you are to Dream. How well did I know her? I knew her best. She played by no ones rules, you know that. She could be the sweetest person, but she was arrogant as hell and hard to get along with. Keyon had been kicking her ass for months when I finally mentioned it to you guys," Shay said.

Her saying that only infuriated Mercedes more.

"Don't say that like we did nothing about it or matter-of-fact. The two of you were close and you knew she was in trouble. So let's try this again," Mercedes said, eyeing Shay to choose her words carefully because that ass was on thin ice.

"We were only supposed to get in this game long enough to make our money and get out. My businesses were suffering and I needed the extra cash, but I never thought things would get out of hand, but you know as well as I did, Diamond believed in taking chances. Once I made my money, I wanted out, but Diamond had one last job she wanted to swing and she promised to get out as well. I had a bad feeling about this last move from the start. And the day that all of this went down, it was all bad," Shay said quietly.

"Where the hell is Keyon?" Mercedes asked.

"He's dead," Shay replied.

"How do you know that," Mercedes asked.

"Trust me, I know. Look there's a lot that I just can't tell you, not by choice and to be honest with you, they're enough people in danger already and I can't take that chance, not again," Shay said.

"What do you mean?" Mercedes eyed her strangely.

"I can't talk about this, Mercedes let it go," Shay said.

"Who you talkin' too? Couldn't be me, because right now I'm a bitch with a real attitude and to inform you, it's not working in your favor, so pump your breaks and let's try this again," Mercedes said calmly.

Mercedes had also noticed that there were two guys that had been watching them since Drew and Dream had departed and they were making her even more uncomfortable. Not being too familiar with her surroundings, she didn't want to make any sudden moves. She called Dream's phone, her and Drew had gone back to their room. Drew asked if she could get a photo of them with her phone and send it to him. He would have someone check them out.

Shay and Mercedes left the restaurant, sure that they had not been followed. She didn't let Shay know what was going on because she was sure she would panic and bring more attention to them. Little did Mercedes know, Shay had already checked them out and she was shaken pretty bad. There was still a lot that she hadn't told Mercedes, but after tonight she knew she had to them everything and that she did.

## THE TRUTH OF IT ALL...

Shay took her time and paced herself, she had to be honest not only with them but with herself. This situation had gotten out of control and before someone else ended up dead, she needed to tell them the real.

Shay told them that Patience and Diamond had been partners. What started out as a few runs had turned into something major. Patience reputation on the streets was suffering, he wasn't on his game and the baby mama was bringing real heat and drama to his ass. Her little drunken rampage in the streets had really caused some static amongst some of the guys he messed with. Dream's world came crashing down all over again as she sat and listened to the truth about her soon to be ex-husband. She found out he wasn't only a cheater and liar, but possibly a murderer as well. Now she understood all of the lies and secrets he had kept from her.

That night on the streets, when Shaunnie and Patience argued, her drunken ass put his business out there. Everything he had told her behind closed doors, she spit it to the bricks. He had discredited a lot of the young dudes he messed with and who looked up to him for being an O.G. He had blown them off as losers and nothing but bitches on the streets, wannabes and they took that personal. Little did he know, Shaunnie had thrown him under the bus and they wanted revenge and they were comin' for him. Patience had protected Dreamer. Diamond was just a casualty of war.

Shaunnie had given Patience a son and she held him over his head. Patience loved his son and he loved her for giving him one and in the mist of it all he dogged his wife, the people he rolled with and part of his family.

As Dreamer sat and listened she became nauseated. Lies have away of resurfacing and when it came to Patience you had to be careful where you stepped. She despised Patience at that moment she didn't know him at all. Their whole life together had been nothing but a lie and the more she listened the more she knew, he had a hand in Diamond's murder.

Here it was two years later and still the mention of Patience's name brought her pain. She had loved him and it seemed as though a part of her always would, but she wasn't going to allow him to continue bringing her down. He had really messed up this time. There were no take backs or do over he would have to face his reality.

Drew held her close as she took in every word. He knew hearing this was only causing her pain, but she needed to hear the truth in order to finally close this chapter of her life. Her heart was breaking and it seemed as though she couldn't escape Patience and his recklessness, she just wanted it all to end and it would be soon. Her hearing was scheduled two days after she returned to the states.

It hadn't dawned on Dream that Shay had said, Patience would do anything to protect her. What had he done, gotten himself into and why would he need to protect her?

"I need some air," Dreamer said.

"You want me to walk with you?" Mercedes asked.

"No, I'm ok. I just need a minute, thanks," Dreamer said.

She looked deep into Drew's eyes, he saw straight through to her soul, she was hurting and there was nothing he could do to ease it all. She kissed him with such tenderness that he wondered if she was kissing him or Patience. For the first time in a while, he felt her love for him was divided, but he had faith in the love they shared.

As if she felt what he was thinking, she assured him he had nothing to worry about, she loved him and that was final.

Dreamer walked along the beach dazed and confused. What had Patience gotten him self into? What did she need protection from? What the hell was going on? She hadn't spoken with him since she receive her letter back, asking her to not contact him again. All of this was surreal, Patience, Diamond, partners, drugs. This whole thing was getting more bizarre by the minute. What had really gone on between Patience and Shaunnie and how did Diamond fit into the equation? None of this was making any sense, but if Shaunnie was involved Dreamer was sure there was some BS in the game, that hood rat had been trouble from the start. Now she definitely proved to be a permanent thorn in Patience's side.

Choices...we all have them and Patience had made some bad ones. Then it hit Dreamer, why was any of this any of her concern? She and Patience were getting a divorce, he was no longer her problem and he had made that clear a long time ago. Knowing the truth about Diamond was all that mattered. She had been murdered and Patience was sitting in jail for it.

"Hey beautiful, you ok?" Drew asked.

Dreamer could always count on him to be there.

"Surprisingly, yes I am," she replied.

Drew was a little surprised by her response.

"Patience isn't my problem anymore, nor is his drama. My concern is finding out the truth about Diamond, plus I have a wedding to plan," Dreamer said with a huge smile.

"Are you sure that your ready for the truth?" Drew asked.

"It's all that matters," she replied.

**"WHAT YOU DON'T KNOW"….**

The four of them met up the next morning in the lobby. Drew and Mercedes filled Dream in on what Shay had shared with them the night before and she appeared to be fine, which worried Mercedes. She was taking this all in stride, what else was there for her to do?

They were meeting with Detectives Brathwaite and Kellman of The Royal Police Force in Bridgetown over on Roebuck Street. For almost three hours they sat and talked about all the speculation surrounding Diamond's death. Dreamer sat and listened without any reaction, Shay showed no surprise in what she was hearing either and Mercedes just wanted to snap.

Jeff and Bruce had been picked up and charged in connection with Diamond's kidnapping and murder and the disappearance of Keyon. His body had been found headless a week after Diamond's disappearance. Kellman said they weren't able to disclose any additional information regarding Jeff and Bruce because even though the case had been officially closed in the states and ruled a drug deal gone back, they were conducting their own investigation because Diamond's body had been found there. In addition to all that they weren't told, they did find out that Jeff had copped a plea implicating Keyon and Patience, the situation continued to go from bad to worse. Patience's name kept popping up and the blame continuously fell in his corner. The more Dreamer heard the more undermined she felt in what she thought she knew about him. She felt she had known him best, but she wasn't sure anymore and she didn't like that feeling. They had been through a lot together and this entire situation had taken her by surprise. Dreamer could never imagine anything like this for

Patience, it wasn't who he was and trying to wrap her mind around it and understand it wasn't helping.

"Hey Bae," Drew said.

"Hey yourself," Dream whispered.

"You don't have to go back in there, you know?" Drew said.

"I know, but I need to do this," she replied.

"If you're tired, let it go. We can do this tomorrow you don't have to take this all on today. We still have another week here and I don't want you trippin' about something that has already happened and you had no control over it," Drew said.

"I am tired and I know Mercedes is on the verge of kicking Shay's ass, I see the way she keeps looking at her. Maybe she can endure this a little more than I can. In the mist of this mess, I still have to find time to plan a wedding. Have I even said thank you?" Dreamer asked.

"For what?" Drew looked puzzled.

"For just being here...always being here. You've been here though everything that has happened and you're the best thing to come out of this for me. How could I not marry or love you? This whole thing has been nothing but a nightmare. Who does this? To be honest with you, I don't think I want to know anymore. Just more unanswered questions and more lies," Dreamer said.

She was drained and it was starting to show. Drew wouldn't admit it, but he would be just as glad to have this all done and over with as well. It would be a breath of fresh air to finally have Patience out of their lives for good.

After spending two weeks in Barbados, they all were no closer to finding out who really murdered Diamond or why, but all the evidence pointed to Patience. Dreamer had found out more about Patience than she really cared to know and signing the divorce papers couldn't happen fast enough. He had distorted everything she had ever known about him and it would be a relief to have this chapter finally come to a close.

She wanted to be rid of any and everything that could possibly remind her of him and the hell he had put her though. He wanted nothing to do with her and that was just fine by her.

The hearing came fast, it was the Wednesday morning after they arrived back home. She had told herself that she was ready to put this behind her. Since he was incarcerated and not able to be at the hearing, Chance had her bring a witness to court to verify the proceedings.

Dream hadn't told Drew about the court date, he had carried her though so much that she felt this was something she had to do on her own. The morning of the hearing she was nervous, nauseated, crying and she couldn't understand why. Were they tears of joy or pain, maybe both?

Chance had asked her to meet him at the courthouse early there were a few things he needed to go over with her before they saw the judge. She would walk away with everything she had when they married, the home, the cars and the condo. All of their finances were in her name and he had no rights to them as well.

The courtroom was filled with people sharing in her pain, but for her she felt alone. Her legs went weak when the judge called her and Chance's name, she stared at him like a deer in headlights, like she was seeing him for the first time. She approached the bench and as she stood there, she could see the judges' mouth moving, but she couldn't hear any words. Mercedes kicked her as she stood there, witnessing the dissolution of her marriage.

"Mrs. Jones, did you hear me? The judge asked. "Mrs. Jones you are here today represented by Attorney Chance Winthrop, of Winthrop, Weinberger and Goodman is that correct?"

Chance nudged her, "Dream, she's talking to you," he said.

"Yes Your Honor," she replied, still she hadn't heard the question.

"Mrs. Jones, how long were you and Mr. Jones married?"

"Fifteen years Your Honor," her words barely a whisper.

"Are there any children to this marriage?"

Dreamer's heart dropped as she thought about her baby, the one she loss, emptiness filled her heart.

"No Your Honor," her eyes filled with tears as pain was written all over her face.

"Mr. Jones is currently incarcerated, is that correct?"

"Yes, Ma'am," she replied.

"Is there anything else in this matter that I should hear before I make my final ruling?" the judge asked.

"Mrs. Jones will maintain her married name, Your Honor," Chance said.

"So be it. Let it be written that today I am granting the dissolution of marriage of one Dreamer Jones and Patience Jones in Pinellas County, Florida's court. So it is written and so it shall be. Have a good day Mrs. Jones," the judge said.

Just that quick, fifteen years were gone, Dreamer felt numb, empty and one again abandoned. Chance asked her to wait for him as they left the courtroom he wanted to give her a certified copy of the divorce.

She stood there in the courthouse in a daze. Chance handed her a copy of the divorce and as she looked into his eyes, words would not come. Mercedes walked with her in silence and for the first time, she didn't know how to comfort her friend or ease her pain. This was almost as worst as the miscarriage she suffered she had fallen into a silent depression. Now Mercedes was afraid of how she would pull things together in order to get past this....

www.ingramcontent.com/pod-product-compliance
Lightning Source LLC
Chambersburg PA
CBHW052149170626
46812CB00004B/1647